If Only

IN MY

Dreams

also by
Michelle Dykman

Her Sanctuary, His Heart

You, Me, and the Stars
BETHEL PRIVATE SCHOOL SERIES | BOOK ONE

Someone Like You
BETHEL PRIVATE SCHOOL SERIES | BOOK TWO

You Found Me
BETHEL PRIVATE SCHOOL SERIES | BOOK THREE

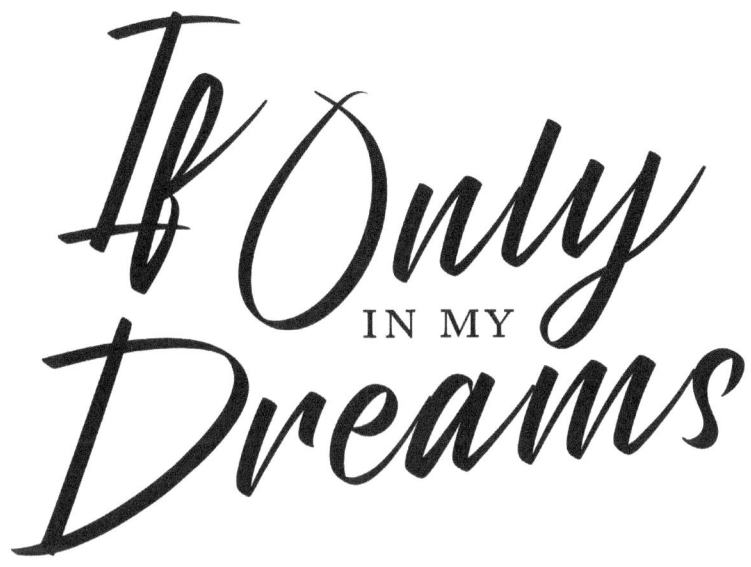

If Only IN MY Dreams

A SNOWY SPRINGS ROMANCE

MICHELLE DYKMAN

AMBASSADOR INTERNATIONAL
GREENVILLE, SOUTH CAROLINA & BELFAST, NORTHERN IRELAND

www.ambassador-international.com

If Only In My Dreams

Paperback ISBN: 978-1-64960-402-6
eISBN: 978-1-64960-451-4
Library of Congress Control Number: 2022947609

Cover design by Hannah Linder Designs
Interior Typesetting by Dentelle Design
Edited by Katie Cruice Smith

Scripture taken from the Holy Bible, New International Version®, NIV® Copyright ©1973, 1978, 1984, 2011 by Biblica, Inc.® Used by permission. All rights reserved worldwide.

AMBASSADOR INTERNATIONAL
Emerald House
411 University Ridge, Suite B14
Greenville, SC 29601, USA
www.ambassador-international.com

AMBASSADOR BOOKS
The Mount
2 Woodstock Link
Belfast, BT6 8DD, Northern Ireland, UK
www.ambassadormedia.co.uk

The colophon is a trademark of Ambassador, a Christian publishing company.

For Jamey, who taught me that there is always light in the darkness.

I would like to thank all the readers who continue to support me as I go along my author journey. I would also like to thank Megan Gerig for helping me look outside the story to best change it within. Thank you to all the people at Ambassador International for their continued support and hard work. Anna Riebe Raats and Katie Cruice Smith, you have made this journey worthwhile. I would like to thank my husband, Jeremy, for your love and support in making this dream a reality and my two sons, James and Noah, Mommy loves you guys, thank you for making my life interesting. Lastly, thank you to my Lord and Saviour Jesus Christ for giving me this tool to spread the good news of You.

When Jesus spoke again to the people, he said, "I am the light of the world. Whoever follows me will never walk in darkness, but will have the light of life."

—John 8:12

Chapter One

"I can't believe you talked me into this."

"Oh, come on, Sarah, where is the 'I'm doing this' attitude you had a few hours ago?"

"I lost it right about the same time you dragged me to the top of this snowy monstrosity. I'm serious, Juliet; I don't think I can do this."

Juliet's tinkling laughter grated like nails on a chalkboard in Sarah Bakker's ears. Skiing was one of the worst ideas Juliet had talked Sarah into trying. She was finally taking the plunge after a morning filled with ski lessons.

"Remember the discussion we had a week ago?"

"Yes . . ."

"What did you promise yourself?"

Sarah sighed. "Self-care."

Juliet's expression filled with compassion. "That's my girl. Okay, Sar-bear, let's hit the slopes."

The ski lift drifted to the top of the mountain, and Sarah's stomach sank deeper. Her hand clenched tighter on the cold metal beside her head. Her ski poles clattered into Juliet's.

"Sorry, these things are so awkward."

"No worries. You'll see. Before you know it, you'll be gliding down the slopes like a pro."

"You have too much faith in me, Juliet."

"And you have too little."

"Perhaps."

"Okay, on three. One, two, and three." Sarah thrust herself forward behind Juliet and landed on the white vista below them. It was breathtakingly beautiful—the white blanket of snow broken by the greens and browns of pine, aspen, and spruce trees. Most of them were covered in a light dusting from the previous day's snow. They shone brightly in the glowing afternoon sun. The cobalt blue sky stretched on forever. The picture was as magnificent as Juliet had promised. The musical sound of laughter intermingled with flashes of color, which blurred past her at a hurried pace. Sarah's stomach churned harder. Was she doing this?

"Deep breaths. You can do this," Juliet whispered. Sarah ripped her eyes from the splendor surrounding her, nervously looking down at her skis. Juliet knew her too well.

Taking another deep breath, Sarah maneuvered after Juliet to the top of the slope. It was the moment of truth.

"This is the green slope, right? The one we checked out at the lodge?" Was that screeching, panicked sound coming from her?

"Sarah, relax. I checked it three times. Now, remember what I told you . . ."

"Yes, yes, poles in hands, arms relaxed, knees bent and skis straight."

"You forgot something . . ."

Another wave of panic. "What?"

"Have fun."

Juliet waited for Sarah to nod. "Good. Now, off we go." Juliet adjusted her ski goggles over her eyes, stamped her skis, and, with her red hair glistening in the bright sunlight, swept gracefully down the long slope.

"Okay, I can do this. I can do this. Remember the little engine that could." *Great, Sarah, quoting children's stories to yourself.* Thrusting her ski poles into the soft snow, she gave a few strong pulls, and then . . . She was flying. A smear of colors and sounds followed her down the long decline. Wild adrenaline pumped through her limbs, filling them with warmth as the cold bit into the exposed skin of her cheeks and nose. Something like euphoria broke through the darkness she'd been fighting for too long. Her heart hammered against her rib cage, and she let out a loud whoop, unable to contain herself. She couldn't believe she was doing this; it was like freedom and joy mixed into a world of colors . . . and— how did she stop again? Oh yes, twist and turn her skis into a triangular shape. Bracing herself with her ski poles and with a tremendous effort, Sarah curled her feet inward. She hoped the force of the movement would stop her downward journey before she crashed into the crowds below. Her skis slowly crossed over each other and brought her to an abrupt halt, planting her face-first in the fresh powder. "Oof."

"SARAH! Sarah, are you okay?" Juliet's alarm might have seemed more genuine if not for the peals of laughter punctuating her words.

"Oh, my word, Sarah"—more laughter—"I wish . . . " She gasped. "I wish you could've seen yourself."

Unsuccessfully trying to stifle her giggles, Juliet braced her arm under Sarah's and hauled her to her feet. Sarah blew the snow from her mouth and wiped her face. Her embarrassment was quickly swept away by awe. "I did it."

Recovered from her laughing fit, Juliet squealed and grabbed Sarah around the shoulders. "See, I told you you could. I mean, isn't it the best feeling in the world? The wind blowing in your hair, the sun on your face—"

"Juliet? Juliet Emerson?" A deep baritone broke into Juliet's rhapsody. They turned to see a tall man with black snow pants and a deep green jacket walking toward them. His wide ski mask and black scarf hid the rest of his features. "And Sarah Bakker. I should have known where the one is, the other would be. I can't believe it; I haven't seen you two since high school."

Juliet raised an eyebrow, and Sarah shrugged. She had no idea who this man was either.

"It's Walters now," Juliet said.

The man unwound the scarf from his face to reveal a pleasant smile. "Walters, as in Callen Walters? The center of the basketball team? I can't say I saw that coming."

"I'm sorry, but who are you?" Juliet asked. Blunt and to the point. Bless her heart.

The man took off his ski goggles and wrapped them lazily around the scarf. Deep green eyes flicked up to them. "I guess I've changed a lot since then." He shrugged. "I'm Lucas Williams."

This attractive man was nothing like the Lucas Sarah remembered from history class. Lucas had transformed from a gangly, skinny kid to a strapping, handsome man.

"Oh, hello. It's good to see you again, Lucas," Sarah said.

"And you. So, do you come here often?"

Juliet sighed and rolled her eyes. "Great, Lucas, where did you get that one? Somewhere in the nineties?"

Lucas laughed. "As a matter of fact, I did."

A smile unwittingly swept over Sarah's face as a wave of nostalgia hit her. High school. Michael. *Don't go there, girl.*

"So would you ladies like to join me for some scintillating conversation and hot chocolate at the lodge?"

"That sounds much better."

Sarah couldn't agree more. "Sounds good. Now if I could just figure out how to get back to the lodge without another embarrassing display of incoordination." Juliet giggled as Sarah shrugged.

Grinning, Lucas unbuckled his skis and dropped them beside his poles. "Here, let me help you," he said and bent to disentangle Sarah's skis. As he stood, he rubbed a small patch of snow from her shoulder and accidentally brushed her cheek. "There, that should help." His touch was pleasant and sent a tiny tendril of something tingling along her skin.

"Thanks. Being a newbie hasn't done me any favors," she said as her face warmed.

Lucas chuckled. "Maybe skiing is like riding a bike. Once you have it, you never lose it."

"Maybe."

"Ready to go again?" Juliet asked.

"That sounds like a great idea. How about we go a few more rounds and meet you, say, in two hours at the lodge?"

"I look forward to it," Lucas said, leaving to rejoin a group of men standing nearby.

Two hours later and with legs aching to the point of exhaustion, Sarah skied back to the lodge. She perked up slightly at the sight of

Lucas waiting for them. He said something to the man beside him and broke off from the group. Juliet grinned and motioned her forward.

"Sarah, why don't you let Lucas help you unbuckle your boots, and I'll meet you at the lodge? Callen said he's waiting there for us."

What was Juliet doing?

"Uh, sure, I don't mind," Lucas said. Was Juliet setting her up?

Sarah shifted uneasily while Lucas unbuckled her skis and motioned for her to step off. Sliding the skis together, he picked up both of their skis and tossed them onto his shoulder.

"Do you mind carrying the poles?" he asked. His green eyes met hers, clear and friendly. Sarah's stomach swooped again. "Ah, yeah, sure." Equipment in hand, Sarah and Lucas walked back to the lodge.

"I'll take care of these," he said as the warm interior of the lodge enfolded them. Sarah handed over the ski poles. Her hand brushed his lightly, and she felt something warm circle her stomach. "Thank you."

"So, I guess I'll see you after I've dropped these off."

"Yeah, sure. I'm just going to change."

Sarah hurried to her room to dispose of her snow gear. The unfamiliar energy inside her was probably from skiing. It was unlike anything she'd ever felt. Smiling at her silliness, she removed her protective clothing and took the elevator back down to the lounge.

Lucas, Juliet, and Callen sat beside a large, marble fireplace, chatting as she entered the room. Lucas rose to his feet. "What can I get you, Sarah?" he asked.

Sarah sank into a large, soft, chocolate-brown sofa opposite Juliet and Callen on a beige loveseat. "Hot chocolate with a candy cane, please." She sighed and stretched out her legs. Her muscles ached from the activity she'd subjected them to earlier.

"Anything else, Juliet? Callen?"

"We're good, thanks," Juliet said.

"Be right back."

"So?" Juliet said as soon as he walked away.

"So, my legs aren't going to thank me in the morning when all this is said and done. But I must admit I had a great time, except for the part where I face-planted into the snow."

Juliet's shoulders shook. "Are you kidding me? That was the best part. So, was I right?"

Despite her misgivings about the whole day, Sarah was having a great time. "Yes, you do know me better than I know myself sometimes; and yes, skiing was a great idea."

Lucas returned, hands ladened with mugs. He was nice-looking. Nothing like Michael, but . . . *Stop it, Sarah. Michael isn't here.* And he never would be again.

"You okay?" Lucas asked. He settled back against the sofa beside her.

"Yes, thanks. Which one is mine?" She pointed to the mugs Lucas had placed on the square, wooden table.

"The reindeer one." He picked up the other mug and leaned back into the sofa. The delicious smell of chocolate and peppermint hit Sarah's nose as she brought the cup up and took a sip. Mmm, much better.

"What did you do after graduation, Lucas?" Juliet said.

"Ah, went to college in Washington, traveled some through the Southern states. I settled for a few years in Montana, but I returned when Grandpa finally decided to retire. I split my time between working the ranch and teaching at the college. What about you, Sarah?"

"Uh, not much. The same—college, home, you know." Much of her life had been about home lately.

"Is there a Mrs. Williams, Lucas?" Juliet asked. What was Juliet going on about now?

Juliet and Callen were happily married, so there was only one reason she would've been asking a question like that. Juliet had made no secret of her desire for Sarah to move on with her life. And in agreeing to go skiing, Juliet had decided to interfere with the other area in Sarah's life that was lacking—her love life.

Lucas' expression became mildly amused. "Ah, no."

"Why not?" *Juliet, please stop.* Her best friend was persistent, like a dog with a bone.

"Never found the time." This time when he shrugged, his arms rubbed against Sarah's, and she forced herself not to react at all, wary of Juliet's watchful eyes. The last thing her best friend needed was encouragement.

"What about you?" Lucas asked, his green eyes focused intently on Sarah.

"Same, too busy." Too heartbroken. Too devoted and too much of a hopeless romantic.

"Well, look at the time. Shall we, honey?" Juliet tugged Callen's hand. "We'll see you two in the morning." Juliet walked out of the room with Callen in tow and left Sarah alone with Lucas.

"That wasn't subtle at all, was it?" Lucas said with a slight chuckle.

Sarah flushed. "I'm sorry. She isn't usually . . . No, she hasn't changed since high school."

"Don't worry. It gives me more time to get to know you again. Would you like to join me for dinner?"

"Are you flirting with me, Lucas Williams?"

"If you have to ask, I must be doing an awful job of it." Lucas rested his back against the arm of the sofa, his hand resting mere inches away from Sarah's shoulder.

"No, you're doing fine. It's me. I'm really out of practice with this sort of thing."

"That's okay. How about we talk while we eat and take it from there?"

Today was about taking chances. "Yes, I'd like that."

They walked together from the sitting room to the dining room beside it. The smell of beef pot pie, rosemary, and something delicious made of sugar lingered in the air, and Sarah's stomach growled in anticipation.

"So, tell me what brought on this sudden urge for adventure?" Lucas inquired after they had been seated. "I mean, the Sarah I remember from school wouldn't be found anywhere near something like a ski slope."

"Under normal circumstances, I wouldn't be, but I made Juliet a promise to try it to add more adventure to my life."

"Tired of waiting with a book?"

Sarah shrugged, so very tired.

Their conversation was interrupted as they placed their orders with the waiter, and before long, they were enjoying a hot meal.

"Do you hike?" Lucas asked and took a bite of his pie.

"I can't say I've ever tried. I usually stick to the pavement—running and biking. I like to be close to home." She didn't mention why, after all these years, she still hoped for him to come home.

"No roughing it?" Lucas grinned, a twinkle of mischief in his eyes.

"No, no camping or anything like that for me. Strictly town life."

"There are some great places near the town that aren't too hard to reach. I'd love to show them to you. Maybe next weekend?"

Goodness, was he asking her out on a date? Anxiety turned her stomach. She'd given up on the very idea of dating or anything on the day she'd rather forget. Something in her expression must've given her away.

"Sarah, if you rather wouldn't, I understand." His words were kind and filled with a knowledge she hadn't revealed. Maybe she was overly sensitive; it was probably nothing.

"How about we stick to talking for now and then see?"

Lucas nodded. "Okay, so tell me what you've been doing since high school."

"That's a long story," Sarah began.

"That's okay. There's still a few hours of night left, and I'm here for the weekend." He took a few more bites of food and settled comfortably into his chair.

"After graduation . . . " Conversation flowed freely through the rest of the main course and to the warm, fudgy brownie she had for dessert. The grandfather clock in the lobby chimed loudly, and Sarah looked up. Almost three hours had passed.

"Before I pass out on you, I think I need to get some sleep."

"Can I meet you for breakfast? I mean, if you want to, of course."

"I'd like that," she said softly. "Good night, Lucas."

"Good night, Sarah. I'll see you in the morning."

Chapter Two

"Could you be more obvious?" Sarah demanded and stormed through the adjoining door of her friend's room. Juliet grinned like a Cheshire cat and unfolded herself from the sofa where she and Callen were watching a late-night TV show.

"You needed a push. I just helped it along. Besides, you must be blind not to notice Lucas was checking you out."

Is that what Lucas had been doing with those long, lingering looks he'd given her while they talked? Color filled her cheeks again, and the knowing grin on Juliet's face grew wide.

"Oh, so you did notice."

"Well, he kind of asked me out. I said I'd think about it."

"Sarah . . ."

"I did agree to meet for breakfast . . . " Juliet's enthusiastic hug distorted anything else she might have said.

"That's great, Sarah. I'm proud of you."

"I didn't agree to a date."

"Maybe not, but you took a step, and that's what this weekend was about, remember?"

Oh boy, did she remember! Breaking out of her comfort zone hadn't seemed so painful when Juliet had suggested the ski trip. Only now did it seem overwhelming.

"Anyway, I think I've had enough excitement for one day. I'm going to take a long, hot bath and then hit the sack."

"Sweet dreams, Sar-bear," Juliet said with another hug.

Sarah hugged her friend tightly and said her goodnight. She closed the interconnecting door and limped to the bathroom.

While the tub filled, Sarah's mind wandered over to a place she kept it from more often than not. She lifted the cold, blue sapphire necklace around her neck and let the memories draw her to another time.

"Merry Christmas, Sarah." Michael's tepid hands reached around her neck and clipped the necklace into place. His eyes sparkled in the dancing light of the candles on the nearby Christmas tree. His soft, brown hair short in a military style.

"Michael, this is . . . It's beautiful, but I . . . "

Michael smiled, his hands moving busily at his sides. "I want to tell you something before I leave, and I'm not quite sure how to say it . . . " He seemed so uncomfortable.

"Is something wrong?"

"At the moment, no, but possibly could be after I say what I need to." He shifted again.

"Michael, you're talking in riddles. Is this another one of your jokes?"

Michael shook his head and chuckled softly. "No, Sarah, what I'm about to say is no joke. In fact . . . " He swallowed hard. Sarah watched his Adam's apple bob up and down. If she didn't know any better, she'd have thought he was nervous. But what did he have to be worried about with her?

"Michael, you're making me nervous. What is it?" she asked, desperate to understand.

His deep blue eyes burned into hers as his warm hands surrounded hers like a cocoon. Tingles raced up her arms. Her heart beat furiously. Michael had never touched her like this. Sure, there were many "my best friend's sister hugs" over the years, but this seemed different, more intimate.

"Michael," she whispered.

"Michael?" Aaron's voice called from somewhere. "Michael," he said again, getting closer.

In a flash, Michael let go of her hands and placed a soft kiss on her cheek. "Merry Christmas, Sarah. See you around." He glanced up at her, his eyes tender and unfathomable. "In here . . . " he said and turned in search of her brother.

That was the last time she'd seen Michael. He'd been deployed the next day, never to be heard from again. What was it that he'd needed to tell her? For months, her hopeless romantic self had thought he finally shared the unrelenting feelings she'd carried for too many years. But as the time went on, she'd come to realize he'd probably meant to let her down easily, having noticed her infatuation with him.

Angry for allowing herself the memory, Sarah flicked off the tap and sank into the delicious warmth of the Epsom salt and lavender-infused bath. Just what she needed. Locking her Michael-centered thoughts back into the far reaches where she kept them, she closed her eyes and let herself relax.

When her fingers were wrinkled and her bones warmed, Sarah lifted herself from the tub and got ready for bed. Not bothering to blow-dry her damp hair, she climbed under the covers and, in a heartbeat, was asleep.

"Ugh, that doesn't look right." *For goodness' sake, Sarah, it's only breakfast.* Why was she fussing over her wardrobe this morning?

She'd hardly packed with dating in mind. The only thing she'd been thinking about when filling her suitcase was lots of snow and keeping warm. Growling under her breath, she snatched a warm, knitted, dark blue sweater and slipped on her jeans. Shoes, hair, and teeth came next.

Purposefully ignoring the mirror, she let herself out of her room and followed the striped carpet into the elevator and back out to the dining room on the ground floor. Juliet and Callen had decided to sleep in today—although Sarah suspected it was more for her to be brave than the need for Juliet to sleep late. Clenching her hands on her writhing stomach, Sarah entered the dining room, quickly spotting Lucas' black hair in the waiting crowd.

"Sarah, over here," he said.

The dining room was alive with excited voices and laughter. The smell of French toast, waffles, and bacon teased her nose, and her stomach grumbled in anticipation. Lucas pulled out the seat beside him and motioned for her to sit down.

"Did you sleep well?" he asked and lifted a large cup of coffee to his lips.

"Like the dead. Who knew skiing would be a cure for insomnia?"

"It certainly does take it out of a person. It still surprises me how well I sleep after a day on the slopes."

"Well, if I ever have to worry about that again, I'll know who to call." Heat filled her cheeks. "I mean, I'll know who to—Oh, never mind."

Lucas chuckled. "I'll hold you to that. Coffee?"

"Yes, please." Signaling to the waiter, Lucas ordered another coffee.

"Are you planning on going out there today?"

"I think so. Juliet says the best way to get rid of the stiffness is to get on in there and ski."

"I have to agree. If you're not opposed to the idea, would you mind if I joined you? You know, to prevent you from landing that pretty, little nose in the snow again."

The heat intensified. "You just had to bring that up. I don't think I'll be going anywhere else but on the green hills. But if your skiing ego can handle a downgrade, you're welcome to come. Besides, I think Juliet and Callen have deserted me."

"How could a guy refuse an offer like that?"

"How, indeed."

Breakfast was enjoyable. Lucas told her some more funny stories about college and the ranch. Sarah found herself laughing until her stomach ached, and she just about choked on her breakfast.

"Are you ready to go?" Lucas asked and wiped his mouth with his napkin.

"Yes. Can I meet you at the equipment rack?"

"Say, in twenty minutes?"

"I'll see you then."

The elevator stopped on her floor with a loud ping. The doors opened just in time for her to see Juliet and Callen walking toward her, hands entwined. One day, she hoped to find a love like that. There was a time she'd dreamed it would be Michael, but now, who knew what the future held?

"Sarah," Juliet said, "where have you been? I checked in your room; you weren't there."

"Actually, I was at breakfast with Lucas. I'm meeting him in a few to go skiing."

Juliet's expression softened, and pride filled it. "My little Sarah all grown up and going on her first date."

"It's not a date, Juliet—just two friends going skiing."

"Whatever you say, my friend. But answer me this. When was the last time you went out with someone who wasn't us or someone from your family?"

True. Since receiving the news Michael was missing in action, presumed dead, dating had held little appeal to Sarah. Amidst the grief and questions, there was no space for a relationship. "You're right."

Juliet hauled her into a hug. "Let yourself live, Sarah," she said. Juliet looked her straight in the eye. "Okay?"

"Okay."

"We'll see on the slopes," Juliet said as she and Callen entered the lift.

Shaking her head, Sarah let herself into the room to clean up. She grabbed her snow gear—making sure to include her goggles, gloves, and scarf—and gently closed the door behind her. A tingle of excitement shot up her spine as she walked down the stairs back to the lobby. Sure enough, Lucas was waiting for her with their gear in hand.

"Are you ready to get on out there?" he asked, repeating her earlier words.

Sarah smiled. Maybe it was time for her to start her new adventure.

Chapter Three

The seat was killing him. Michael shifted uneasily in the passenger seat of Levi's red F-150. Its gray interior was nice but too soft, like he would disappear into it at any moment. Light cotton rubbed against the freshly healing scars on his upper body. Dark trousers covered his pale, atrophied-muscled legs. After three years in the dry, dusty plains of Afghanistan, the Denver skyline's sprawling scape was strange, intimidating. The tires whirred sleekly against the black asphalt, so different from the rough, rocky ground he knew. He pumped his clenched fist; the action helped to calm the anxiety clawing at his throat.

"You okay?" Levi asked.

The concern in his inquiry grated against Michael's calm. How many times in the last hours had Levi asked him that question? Ten? Twenty? Each question chipped into the tiny bit of sanity to which Michael tenuously held. The truth was he didn't know if he'd ever be okay. The dream he'd held onto with nail-biting tenacity was now his reality. Yet the clutches of his enemy still clung to him like angry hooks buried in his bleeding skin.

"I'm fine, Levi. Please stop asking. I'm tired, and . . . " He blew out a breath, silencing the scream that pushed to escape his throat. The bone-deep weariness in his body had little to do with lack of sleep. After surviving for years stuck between fight or flight, his body didn't know how to rest. Torture, lousy diet, and sleep deprivation would do that to any sane man. The nightmare may be over in the daylight, but at night, it haunted what little peace he'd managed to find.

"Sorry," Levi said, concern filling his voice. After all, wasn't that what pastors did? Worry too much about everyone?

Levi nodded. Michael leaned back against the headrest and followed the patterns of cars and buildings as they drove further through the city. It all looked so different, or maybe he was different. He wasn't the same man who'd left Fort Carson with stars in his eyes so long ago. Closing his eyes, he drew a few breaths in through his nose and out his mouth. The therapist in Germany said it would help. At times, the sequence stopped the attack. And other times, all he could do was hold on and ride it out until eventually, spent with sweat, he passed out. He wished he hadn't agreed to stay with his parents. Still, he had nowhere else to go after his honorable discharge from the military.

"We're almost there," Levi said.

Another wave of anxiety hit Michael. For years, he'd ached for his family, missing them with a fierceness that made him all the more determined to survive his ordeal. How would they react to seeing him? A son returned from the dead. What would he say to them? His gut churned harder, nausea welling in his throat. Swallowing hard, he drew the sequence of breaths again.

Abruptly, the car came to a halt, and Michael opened his eyes and glanced around him with interest.

"We're here?"

Levi's forehead dipped into a deep frown as he shook his head. "We're about fifteen minutes out. You look like you're going to hurl. Are you sure you can handle this?"

The lie or the truth? Levi would catch him out, anyway. "I don't know." It burned his gut to admit it after everything—admitting weakness chaffed against the very rules he'd enforced to survive.

A rough hand landed on his shoulder, and he winced at the impact.

"We're here for you, man. A lot has changed while you've been away. Mom and Dad might not be the people you remember; your captivity wore them down almost to the end. Please try to remember how much they love you."

Levi had unwittingly put into words the concerns that churned in Michael's chest. How much would his return cost those around him? His brother turned back into the slow-flowing traffic as Michael fought against his rising despair. The day the army hauled his sorry self out of the dark hole of his captivity, Michael had fought to see his family. First, no one had been allowed to see him until he could at least stand on his own two feet. Then there were the weeks of debriefing and psychological counseling he'd had to endure. Finally, when three more months had passed, Michael was allowed to go home. Levi was there the hour he'd landed. Noah stayed home to prepare the family, and Drew brought the food. Or so he'd been told. Perhaps everything wasn't that different.

"Did someone call Aaron?" He didn't dare think of her. Wherever that ship had been going, it had sailed long ago.

"Yeah. Noah did. As soon as we heard."

"That's good. I hear Ben found his courage and made an honest woman out of Susie."

A glimmer of a smile lit Levi's face. "It took much prayer and prodding. They're expecting their first any day now."

"And Emma—I thought you two would be married by now?"

The smile disappeared. "It didn't work out," Levi said sadly.

"Want to talk about it?" Anything to distract him from himself.

"Nothing much to say. It's in the past, and I've accepted that this is what God wanted for me. Someday, I'll know why."

God. Another gray cloud moved over him, and he was immersed in memories. Nights of sobbing in desperation, his broken body wracked with hunger and pain. Days of waiting, hoping, praying. Where was God in all he'd suffered?

The lock of his memories snapped as they turned the last corner and came to a gentle halt outside a medium-sized, blue house. Three steps led up to the front door, and a neat porch wrapped around the one side. A large fir tree covered a long, rectangular window on the other side.

"You ready?" Levi asked.

Let's hope. His answer died on his lips as the white door of the house flew open and the familiar faces of his parents and brothers tumbled out. Keenly observing the change in his parents, Michael unfolded his battered body, barely suppressing a wince. He'd taken two steps when a melee of arms wrapped around him, and a din of desperate words and tears surrounded him, rapidly overwhelming the fragile hold on his sanity.

"Thank God, our boy is home. God is good," his father said, his gravelly voice husky with emotion. Warmth filled his chest; his eyes grew misty. His slack arms wrapped around his parents' trembling frames, and he held on for dear life. He was home.

"Mom, Dad, it's good to see you." He squeezed out past the hard lump in his throat. *Help.*

Levi caught his eye and nodded. "Why don't we give Michael a bit of space?"

"We never gave up hope," his mother said and hugged him tightly. Thankfully, it was short; his sore body couldn't take much more.

Gradually, the crowd dispersed and went one by one back inside the house. Michael leaned against the hood of Levi's truck, gulping air against the wild beating of his heart. When his heart rate slowed, Michael pushed himself up and went to join his family, pausing for a moment to thank Whomever was out there he'd made it back.

Out of instinct, Michael ducked as a loud clatter of something came from the kitchen. Noah sat down opposite him on his parent's old, floral love seat. "It's okay; Mom dropped a casserole dish." Michael nodded and sat up, embarrassed by his lack of control. "Dad sent me in here to check on you."

"I'm okay, Noah. Just tired."

"Mom says we'll be ready in a few hours. Why don't you lay down in the guest room until then?"

"Yeah, want to show me the way?" His parent's home in Denver looked similar to the one in Snowy Springs. Still, everything about it felt wrong, different, strange—and just about any other negative emotion he could muster. The hallway grew dark as Noah led Michael up the stairs and to a room with the door closed. As he opened it, the past sucked him in. It was a distant past, one that had happened long before Afghanistan. With brutal force, his captors had ripped that past from him.

A tall bookshelf with four shelves sat opposite the doorway, memories portrayed in baseball trophies, photo frames, and books. The walls were a pale gray, and the wide bed at the center was covered in the same comforter that had been on his bed in Snowy Springs. If he were a gambling man, he'd guess his clothes hung in the closet in the left corner.

"This is how Mom held onto you," Noah said.

Michael took the photos into his hands one by one as Noah quietly exited the room. He tried without success to remember what his life was like then. Laying back on the soft coverlet, Michael held up the dark, wooden-framed picture. The photo was of the Thomas and Bakker families on the day Michael and Aaron had graduated from high school. Sarah stood shyly at his side, his arm wrapped around her shoulders. It was a friendly gesture then, but not long afterward, his feelings for Sarah had begun to change. Once again, he regretted not being honest with her that Christmas Eve.

It's too late now. Michael lay the photo face-down on the bed beside him and closed his eyes. The house's muted noises gradually faded as sleep took him to the place where the nightmares waited.

"Move back, soldier. I'm going to blow the lock."

Shaking knees buckled, and he stumbled back further into the cell. A loud bang chimed in time with the continued barrage. Michael shrank back as the shadow loomed over him.

"Don't worry, soldier; we're here to get you home."

"Michael . . . "

"Michael . . . "

The violence of the nightmare disappeared as the light penetrated his eyes.

"Michael, man, can you hear me?"

In an instant, he was back in his room—no, not in his room. Somewhere familiar.

"Levi? What . . . Wait . . . Where am I?"

"You're at Mom and Dad's house in Denver."

Michael pushed himself up to sitting and rubbed his trembling hands along his face. They were wet.

"Where were you?" Levi asked.

"The cell." Air heaved in and out of his lungs in time with the racing of his heart. Droplets of sweat slid down his arms and pooled between his clenched fists. The fresh smell of wood and his mom's cooking was nauseating and comforting in equal measure. Levi sat down beside him.

"At the risk of repeating myself, I'll ask anyway. What happened to you?"

The clock on the bookshelf ticked over and over again, and Levi waited patiently beside him.

"It was bad," he whispered.

The patience on Levi's face folded into pain and then into compassion. "I'm sorry, man."

Michael nodded, knowing that no one could help. The counselor at the base had told him; eventually, the memories wouldn't have the power they held now. With time, he would heal. Michael didn't believe him.

"I'll give you a few minutes. Mom sent me up to tell you dinner's ready."

"Thanks. I'll be down soon." The door closed with a soft click. For a long time, Michael stared at the bookshelf one by one, closing down the memories. That Michael was dead, and that was all there was to it. He flicked the light on in the adjoining bathroom and splashed cold water over his hot face. Bracing his hands on either side of the sink, he stared into the mirror, desperately looking for something. Maybe he was looking for someone, but that someone was no longer there. Sighing, he dried his face and hands and left the room.

The dining room was oddly quiet as he entered. His father sat in his place at the head of the table ladened with every food Michael loved growing up. Bless her, his mother had made macaroni and cheese. Mom sat to the left of his dad, Drew to his right, and Noah beside Drew. Seeing the familiar pattern, Michael cracked a smile, and the room around him relaxed. He took his place beside his mom, followed by Ben and Susie. The familiar sight warmed a cold, lost piece inside him. Almost like he was coming back to life. For him, though, everything had changed. Everyone held hands as his father blessed the meal, and without preamble, they dug in.

"Ben, how is the rodeo going?" Drew asked.

Michael stopped chewing. Was Ben in the rodeo? When had this happened?

"It's going well; looking forward to the off-season when Susie and I can spend some quality time together before the baby arrives."

Drew nodded and peppered Levi with questions about the church. The gap he'd left was barely noticeable. It was like that movie where the ghost watched the family living their lives with no knowledge of him there. Today, he felt like that ghost—out of place, invisible. Being with his family was a lot harder than he'd imagined it would be.

"Michael, would you like some more macaroni?" his mom asked. Her gentle smile reminded him of what love looked like. Another piece warmed.

"No thanks, Mom. I'm good."

But as the time passed, each sound, smell, and scrap of stainless steel against ceramic screeched like the cry of an eagle in his ear. The combined cacophony of six voices echoed like booming canons on his already-frazzled nerves. Light-colored walls came closer and closer and stole what little oxygen circulated the room.

"If you'll excuse me," he muttered. Desperation thundered in him as he pushed out his chair. He needed air; he needed space. He needed to get out of there. Feet beating on the wooden floor, he ran out of the room, out the front door, and into the open space behind the house gasping for breath. Bright sunlight and frigid cold slapped his exposed cheeks and hands and slowed his frantic flight. For the second time that day, his chest heaved in need of oxygen. Squeezing his tired eyes closed again, he feasted on it.

An overturned crate stood beside what he assumed was the shed, and Michael gingerly sat on it. He balanced his elbows over his bent knees and soaked in the peaceful silence. His family was worried about him. And why wouldn't they be? He could feel their eyes watching him from the nearby house. They'd probably drawn straws, and one brave soul would come to check on him. The door creaked open, and a set of boots walked down the steps toward him.

"Michael?" Levi asked. "Are you okay?"

Would he ever be? "Yeah, I guess."

"Why don't you come on back in? Mom's worried. We all are."

He nodded but didn't move from his seat.

With a sigh, Levi turned and headed back to the house.

The sun began to dip below the horizon, and the cold sank deep into his bones. Michael had no choice but to brave the house again. How was he going to get through this? Levi would say pray; God would help him out. Michael didn't think so. The warm house beckoned to him and promised love, family, and hot cocoa. Man, please let him not screw it up.

Bracing his wayward emotions, Michael pushed to his feet and followed Levi back into the arms of his smiling family.

Chapter Four

"You and Lucas have been seeing a lot of each other this week," Juliet said.

Sarah left her coffee on the table between them. The slow afternoon traffic ebbed past Delmonte's Bakery and Coffee Shop on Main Street of Snowy Springs.

"We only had coffee a few times."

Juliet rolled her eyes. "By a few times, you mean every day this week, don't you?"

"Yes, but just as friends."

"So, you're not seeing him again this weekend?"

Heat filled Sarah's cheeks. "Actually, he asked me to go hiking with him tomorrow."

"See? What did I tell you? Dating."

"I'm doing no such thing. Okay, maybe. It's still so new, and . . . " Sarah shrugged. "I'm scared."

Compassion filled Juliet's eyes. "I think it's great that you've taken a chance to put yourself out there. I know how hard this must be for you."

Juliet didn't need to mention Michael for them to know she was referring to him. Michael was her past. She'd loved him for so long that the thought of dating, let alone loving another man, had never crossed her mind. But like all things, it was time to put away the sackcloth and embrace the present.

"So, hiking . . . "

Her conversation with Juliet was still fresh in her mind the next day. Sarah blew out a deep breath.

"Are you nervous?" Lucas asked and gestured to the path they would be hiking. A long, snow-covered way stretched out into the distance between tall, green spruce trees. Sarah pressed her mittened hands to her stomach and hoped the battalion of ants inside would stop marching for a minute.

"I think so. Are you sure this is the only way to the top?" It seemed so far, and the last thing she wanted to do was make a fool of herself.

Lucas smiled. "Sarah, I promise it's an easy walk, and the scenery is beautiful. You won't regret giving it a try." He gazed at her, his green eyes soft and kind.

"Are you sure?"

Lucas' mouth twitched. "Can I tell you something?"

"Does it have something to do with climbing that?" Sarah asked.

"No, nothing to do with the hike." He waited for her to join him on the path. "I wanted to ask you out in school."

Sarah stumbled over an overgrown root, almost face-planting once again in the snow. "What!" Had she heard him right? "Why didn't you?"

The stiff snow crunched under Lucas' boots as he leaned against a nearby tree with a faraway expression. "Michael Thomas."

Sarah's heart gave an involuntarily thud at the sound of his name. "I saw the way you looked at him. I knew he was too blind to notice . . . " He shrugged. "So, I didn't."

Something cold inside Sarah thawed. "I'm glad you decided to now. Michael was a teenage dream, and I did love him."

"But not now?" Lucas' smile dimmed.

Sarah's heart lurched again. "I'm working on it. That part of me will always love Michael. But he will never be in my life again, and I have accepted that. I'm ready to move on. Besides, I've very much enjoyed our time together."

Lucas smiled, his eyes crinkling as it spread over his face into a beautiful expression. Goodness, he was handsome. "Me, too. So then, would it be okay to say that I would like to take you to dinner tonight?" Oh, he was sharp.

"How about if I survive this hike, I'll agree to go to dinner with you?"

"Then I guess we better get started." Lucas laughed and held out his gloved hand to her.

She took it and allowed him to pull her further up the path. The butterflies still danced inside her, but somehow, they felt a bit more stable when her hand was in his.

Sarah's boots crunched into the snow, her footprints uncovering pine needles and cones and various other plant life covered generously by white fluff. The winter in Colorado was beautiful; the snow came early and left late. Winter was Sarah's favorite season. Perched beside a fire with a hot cup of cocoa and a good book rated amongst one of the biggest highlights in Sarah's life.

"So, why did you decide on teaching? I mean, before you came back to ranch with your dad?" she asked.

They'd hiked about halfway into the trail. Now and then, Lucas would stop and point out a bird or a small animal print and tell her how they fit into their ecosystem and helped their environment. It was fascinating to hear him talk about a topic he loved.

Lucas' smile grew. "When I was growing up, I always wanted to be an engineer. However, during my internship, I discovered how much more good I could do if I taught engineers instead of being one. It was kind of like that proverb, 'Give a man a fish, and you feed him for a day; teach him to fish, and you feed him for a lifetime.' I thought that if I could train people to be engineers but also be conscientious of the world around them, then I could help preserve the earth in some small way."

"That's how I feel about history. Learning from the past to preserve the future."

"So, you're a history teacher then?"

Sarah shook her head, trying to explain. "When I was in school, the only job I ever wanted was to be a history teacher or professor. I imagined myself going on archeological digs and discovering wondrous, new treasures. In my first semester at Penn State, Avery was in a car wreck. We almost lost her."

"Avery, your older sister?" he asked.

Sarah nodded and continued, "I came home to help her around the house and ended up staying. I completed my undergrad online and signed up for my master's while working at the library. It didn't work out. The week I was due back at the university, my mom had a bad fall. She needed someone to help at the bookshop; and then my dad passed, and, well, here I am."

Lucas frowned, compassion lining his eyes. "I'm sorry, Sarah. I heard about your dad; I'm sorry for your loss. I wish you would have been able to fulfill your dream."

Sarah shrugged; since they'd lost Michael, her dreams had changed. Everything about her life seemed to have changed.

"My dreams are different now. More realistic." Nothing brought reality into perspective more than the loss of a loved one.

Lucas turned to her and took her hands into his again. "You deserve to be happy, too, Sarah."

"Boy, you sound just like Juliet." Sarah gently tugged her hands out of his, suddenly self-conscious.

"Then I must be right." Lucas laughed. Those gorgeous eyes twinkled as they looked down at her.

Sarah's stomach dipped and swooped again. She stifled a nervous giggle. "You remember Juliet very well."

"How could I not? She's a part of you." His innocent statement robbed Sarah of breath. Lucas seemed not to notice because he continued to speak. "I remember a few times coming around the corner and hearing Juliet say she was always right about something or other." Lucas laughed again.

Her shoulders shook as they continued down the trail. Lucas remembered so many things about her from school, and she remembered so little about him.

"At the risk of sounding like a five-year-old, are we there yet?" she asked. The trees had grown thicker around them; the vivid greenery mixed with white closed in and blocked out the waning afternoon sun.

Lucas stepped out ahead and quietly beckoned to her, finger on his lips. Sarah tip-toed closer, a fuzzy, warm feeling uncurling in her as Lucas wrapped his arm around her back and pulled her into his side. He was pointing at something. Just ahead of them stood a mama deer with her baby nearby in an open meadow. Both peacefully browsed on the nearby flora, their soft brown and white fur blending with the trees and earth.

"Wow," Sarah whispered. Being this close to Lucas was nice. The warmth of him was solid against her. So, when his arm tightened slightly and drew her in front of him, she didn't resist.

"I know, right? I hoped the deer would be here today. I hiked here earlier in the week and found the mama. Aren't they beautiful?"

"Yes, they are. I don't think I've ever seen one in the wild before."

Sarah's hands trembled as she rested them over his, wrapped around her stomach. Her emotions were a jumbled mess. She liked Lucas. And it was evident that he wanted a relationship with her. But as much as she tried to suppress it, she still longed for those arms to belong to someone else. Yesterday, she'd made a promise to herself to embrace her time with Lucas; so despite the protest of her heart, she would. The air grew colder as they watched the deer until the mama and her baby faded into the darkness of the forest.

With a loud sigh, Lucas let her go. "I think I'm about ready for some hot chocolate. What do you say?"

"That sounds wonderful. Where are we going?"

"If you don't mind, there's a place about ten minutes from here where we could grab some lunch."

More time with Lucas, how could she say no? "I'd like that. Thank you."

The walk down the trail took them less time. Sarah found herself enthralled by the wealth of Lucas' knowledge about the history of the park and the town. It was lovely to have a conversation with someone who shared a passion with her.

Before long, they were walking into a quaint restaurant a few feet from the park.

"What kind of hot chocolate would you like?" Lucas asked as they sat in a booth in the middle of the restaurant.

An elderly lady came from behind the counter to pour thick, hot liquid from a colossal urn. Seeing Lucas, she greeted him by name.

"I come here often," he said sheepishly.

Sarah snickered. "What kinds do they have?"

"Well, there is caramel, peppermint, cranberry, and, if you're adventurous, blackberry."

"I think I'll stick with peppermint."

"Are you sure? The cranberry is pretty good."

Be adventurous, Sarah. "Why not? Let's try that cranberry, then."

His eyes crinkled at the sides as he stood, brushing her shoulder as he passed her. Sarah was giddy. She pressed her hands to her stomach; the buzzing there wound into a frenzy. There'd always been nervous excitement when Michael was with her, but this was something entirely different. Was it because she knew his intentions? Or was it because she was beginning to feel something for him?

No closer to an answer, Sarah took out her phone and checked her email; it gave her a break from her confused thoughts.

After a short while, Lucas returned with their hot chocolates. He placed the cups and two thick chicken salad sandwiches on the table.

"I thought you might be hungry," he said and took his seat.

"Are you kidding? I'm starving. Thank you."

"You're welcome. How are you feeling after the hike?"

"Great. Like I could conquer the world. Thank you, Lucas; it was an unforgettable experience."

"I hoped it would be. Dig in; there's more than enough."

They finished up their food and drink and climbed into the car for the journey back.

"Are we still on for tonight?" he asked with the cutest expression of hopefulness she'd ever seen. They were outside her house. "Yeah, I'm looking forward to it."

"Great, I'll come to get you in"—he checked his watch—"three hours?"

"That'll give me enough time for a nap and a long, hot bath. Thank you again for today. I enjoyed it more than I thought I would."

"I'm glad." He squeezed her hand, ran around the car, and opened the door for her.

He watched her quizzically for a moment as she stood outside the car, and then he stepped forward, the decision made. Gentle hands took hers and drew her into his chest to hug her. "I look forward to seeing you later." The blunt honesty in his words melted her heart a little further.

"Me, too."

Sarah took time to admire the freshly falling snow as he drove away. She'd always loved the snow. Dainty, white flakes floated leisurely to the ground in windswept patterns. It was like a promise of something new and refreshing. She took a deep breath and walked up the steps into the bungalow.

The small, two-bedroomed, white building she'd bought when her position at the library had become permanent was perfect for her. Each room was decorated to her unique and colorful taste. A wooden front porch was decked with large, round pillars and huge, square windows on either side of her deep brown door. It was her home and her haven. The door closed with a gentle flick of her foot, and she was glad she'd remembered to turn up the heat before leaving.

Would she be too silly to do a little happy dance? No, she would not.

Chapter Five

The droning chaos of the mall surrounded Michael. He walked faster. *Come on, come on.* Noah, Drew, and he were on a mission to find a present for his mother's birthday. Despite his insistence that it wasn't a good idea, Noah and Drew insisted it would mean the world to their mother if he would go with them. After hiding out in his room for the past week, it was the least Michael could do. In the daytime, life went on; but at night, he would find one of them outside his room, pacing, waiting for the next nightmare to strike. He knew they loved him; he just wished he could be more deserving of that love. Nighttime was his enemy, one he'd imposed unwittingly on his family without a clue on how to keep his foe to himself.

Another person stumbled into him, and he clenched his fists. His body tensed, one step closer to a breaking point. Ignoring the two men a short distance away, he headed for the nearest exit. The silence of the parking garage sounded much better than the din of shoppers. Maybe he'd be able to calm down before they'd figured out he'd gone.

Michael absorbed the dank silence among the cars. It was quiet and reminded him eerily of his prison. Drawing a deep breath, he suppressed another wave of paralyzing terror. Whirring faintly, the tailgate of Noah's truck lowered. Michael hopped on, exhausted.

A muffled vibration in his pocket broke the silence, and he silenced it without a second glance. His brothers were onto him; they'd be here soon. Cursing, he hung his head. Time. He needed a moment of quiet serenity to gather his thoughts, to not feel like a freak, to curb the impulse to strike with maximum force any innocent bystander in his path.

"Ready to head home?" Noah asked, followed closely by Drew.

Michael's head lifted. Both were empty-handed. Great, another thing he'd blown.

"Look, this was a bad idea." How long would it take for them to see? He was no longer the Michael they knew. Two sets of blue eyes met him, both filled with questions and compassion. Fragments of his time overseas were the topic of many discussions over the past week. His nightmares filled in the rest. Would this ever be over?

The loud screech of tires strained his already taut nerves. Before a conscious thought crossed his mind, he curled into a tight ball. Tension hummed through his body.

"Mike, it's okay."

He snapped. "Don't you see it will never be? I will never be okay. Please take me home."

Hands clenched his hair, and he collapsed back into the truck bed. No tears came; then again, he didn't remember how to cry. His hands continued to shake as he stared at them. He didn't know how much longer he could do this. A danger to the world during the day and more so to his family at night, he needed to leave for everyone's sake.

Drew and Noah climbed into the truck with out another word, and after a time, so did he. The journey home was a silent one. As the truck pulled to a stop outside the house, Michael ran before Noah and Drew had disembarked. The bedroom door slammed shut, and he paced the five steps it took to get across the room. There was no other choice. He had to leave.

With a quick movement, the phone was up at his ear and ringing. "Aaron, do you have a place for me to stay?"

"Yeah, man, ready when you are."

"Thanks, man. I owe you. I'll be there before the end of the week."

Sweet relief. Soon, he'd be away from Denver and the expectations he couldn't hope to meet. Michael flopped down onto the couch after his mom chased him out of the kitchen. Michael wished they'd let him help; he'd been itching to do something for months. Sitting around was slowly driving him crazy. The mind-numbing fear he carried was slowly drilling him deeper into the black.

"Where are you going?"

"How did . . . " Levi was scary sometimes. "Never mind, back to Snowy Springs. Aaron has a place I can stay. He says I can help out there until I find my feet."

Levi took the single-seater opposite him. "Are you sure that's a good idea?"

"You mean, a better idea than exploding at every opportunity? Being a danger to Mom and Dad? Not to mention the other stuff," Michael said bitterly.

"Wouldn't it be better just to stay here in Denver and get help?"

"I can't. This place is suffocating me, Levi." He needed clean, open-air, quietness; he couldn't explain his urge to leave Denver. Everything—people, noise, dangers—compounded the likelihood he would do something stupid—or worse, get someone killed.

He squeezed his eyes shut; even then, he could not erase the carnage that would follow such a decision. In the desert, it was so simple. Get home. It was his one driving goal, the very desire that gave him purpose. But now that he was, the prize was nothing like he'd imagined. He was nothing like he imagined, and he wasn't sure he ever would be again.

"When will you tell them?"

"Soon. Tonight, perhaps."

"Don't wait too long. You've been gone a long time; let them have some time to have you back."

"I'll try."

Chapter Six

A straight jacket felt better. He would know. The dark blue suit sat unnaturally against his skin with its shiny material and tight pants. According to Drew, they were the latest style. Whatever. What did Michael know about fashion? He lived in a uniform. The pillowy softness of the beige leather reminded him of a squishy marshmallow. Why had he allowed his brothers to persuade him to come tonight? An environment such as this one was an incident waiting to happen.

Soft candlelight gave the ritzy restaurant an expensive ambiance. The classical tinkle of piano keys added to it. Waiters in stiff black and white uniforms moved with practiced ease around the people-filled booths. How had Drew managed to wangle reservations to this place? Via de la Mia lived up to every bit of lavish luxury its name implied.

"Relax, dude. Enjoy a night of Denver's finest before you cloister yourself into small-town life again." Drew thought he was nuts to move back to Snowy Springs. He loved Denver. The lights, theaters, and restaurants—basically, the high life he'd wished for when they were kids.

In the aftermath of Michael's capture, an exodus of the Thomas family members from Snowy Springs had begun. First, Levi accepted a new church call, and his parents soon followed. At last, Drew and Noah uprooted, too. Ben and Susie traveled a lot with the rodeo circuit and visited when they were in town. No one wanted to remain with the memories of what was lost, which made it even more so strange to them that he wanted to go back.

"Yeah, yeah, whatever," he muttered. He allowed his mind to wander back to the earlier conversation he'd had with his parents.

"Mom, Dad, I'm going back to Snowy Springs," Michael said.

His mother let out a small sound, and his father covered her hands with his. "If this is what you feel is best for you, Michael. We are behind you one hundred percent."

Michael sighed. "This city is too big and loud. I hope in Snowy Springs, I can find some peace, some healing." It sounded so lame. Like an excuse.

His father's eyes filled with compassion. "We're so glad you are back, son, and we pray for you every day."

Silent tears ran down his mother's face as Michael embraced her. "I love you, Mom," he said. His mother clutched him tightly, her words muffled by the folds of his shirt. He released her and embraced his dad. "Thank you. I'll come back as soon as I can."

Despite his best efforts, civilian life had turned out to be more grueling than basic training. *Just get through tonight, Michael.* His mantra. The phrase hurled him back to a dark place. Energy leaked out of his body, and the heavy oppression of the last three years overwhelmed him. His back burned from remembered lashings. All noise drowned out by heated shouts in Pashto or soft murmurs in Dari. There was no distinction between the people, though. One destroyed; the other healed. Again and again. *Please, please.*

"Michael? Michael? Are you here?"

He snapped back to the present; his gaze bounced wildly from one brother to the other and met their worried expressions. "I'm okay."

"Do you want to leave?" Levi asked. He ignored the disgruntled looks thrown his way. Ben's idea of the rodeo sounded better and better by the minute. Anything would be better than embarrassing himself again with his uncontrolled moods. Reality crept in as his heart rate slowed to normal. He was in Denver. The desert was far away. He was safe; he was home.

"Yeah, sorry. Phased out there for a second." A second that felt like an eternity.

"I'd say there is a lot more to it than that," Levi said. "You were miles away, Michael . . . "

Michael held up his hand. "I'm *okay*." Curse Levi for his all-knowing pastoral stuff. Out of the brothers, Levi was the most aware of how broken Michael was, except Noah. Noah carried his demons. Frustration and sadness covered Levi's expression. "Still stoic, I see."

Michael rolled his shoulders, unable to deny Levi's claim. "I'm fine, Levi." Levi at least had the wisdom to back off this time. There'd been a few close calls in the past days. Guilt and sorrow chewed his gut at the expression on his brother's face. He'd missed his family, but he needed to protect them, even from himself.

"What are we doing for Mom and Dad's anniversary?" Drew asked.

Thank goodness for the safer topic. Maybe when the weight of his guilt and shame was behind him, he'd be able to relax. Michael opened the menu and purposefully held it in a way that blocked his view. He needed a few moments to himself.

"I recommend the ballet. Mom's always wanted to go," Noah said.

"Really, you would do that to Dad?" Levi answered.

"Ah, come on, you know he'd do anything for her. So yeah, I think the ballet is a good idea. Michael, what do you think?" Levi looked pointedly at him.

Oh, he was talking to him? "Yeah, sure," he muttered. Silence again. Michael lowered the menu; three sets of blue eyes were on him.

Levi sighed. "Bro, could we get more than a yeah out of you?"

Michael bristled. What did Levi expect from him? Sunshine and roses? The compassion in Levi's eyes deflated his intended tirade.

"I'm sorry," he said at last. "Remind Dad to get flowers, and I'm sure Mom will enjoy the ballet."

There was an audible sigh of relief as the tension around the table subsided.

"We love you, man." Drew tapped him on the shoulder; Noah sat back into his chair, nodding.

The conversation continued and jumped from one topic to the next. Drew had a new job in Colorado Springs. Noah would be stationed at Fort Carson, transferred to a desk job after the surprise attack that almost destroyed their unit. Levi was training a new youth pastor. His church had grown so much in the time Michael was away that he needed the help. Michael envied the peace Levi carried with him, the surety. Faith had once meant something to Michael, but months and months of hardship had snuffed out that blazing ember. God had abandoned him when Michael had needed Him the most. What kind of a loving God left one of His own in a small, white solitary box of concrete until, by a stroke of luck, they'd found him? What kind of a God watched His own be tortured day after day? No, God didn't exist as far as Michael was concerned.

"Are you ready to order?" Drew asked.

"Where's the mac and cheese?" Michael asked.

The droll question had the desired effect; a collective groan circled the table.

"Really, Mike? We're at a high-end Italian restaurant, and you're asking for mac and cheese? Did you lose your ability to eat fine food in the desert?" Drew was a foodie. He knew all the best and upcoming places to eat. To him, asking for macaroni and cheese at this restaurant was the same as burning the flag.

Michael froze again. He forced himself to relax and smile. "Well, when all you get is moldy bread, mac and cheese sounds pretty good to me. And I'm sure it doesn't cost as much as a used car. Honestly, Drew, what were you thinking? This place looks like it costs more than I make in three months!"

"This place just happens to serve the best ravioli in the state."

"Sure, what do they put inside? Gold?" Noah asked.

Michael high-fived him. He was relieved to see Levi crack a smile.

"I'm not sure; I'd have to ask the waiter," Drew deadpanned.

The brothers laughed and got back to their menus. Now that he was here, Michael knew what he'd been missing. His family, his brothers, and the familiarity of home. It was good to be back.

Before long, their food arrived. Drew had ordered for him, and Michael was happy to see a mac and cheese version called something-or-other-Italian placed in front of him. He took a bite. The food was delicious.

"See, I told you so," Drew said. "You're gonna miss out on all this wonderful food and wait until you see where we're going next."

"Next?"

"We're going to show you all you're going to miss out on in Snowy Springs." Drew high-fived Noah and laughed.

Michael glanced over at Levi in time to see his eyes roll. Levi was on the same page. A night on the town was not his idea of fun.

The talking around the table stalled as something to the left grabbed Levi's attention.

"Hey, look who's here, Michael!" Levi's face lit up like a Christmas tree, and a wide grin appeared on his face.

Michael paused mid-bite and followed Levi's gaze. Surprise the size of a two-by-four smacked into him. His memories had lied to him.

Sarah Bakker.

She was so much like he remembered and so different. Her long, brown hair shone in waves down her slim back. She seemed delighted with the man who stood by her side. There was something familiar about him. Michael quickly dismissed him. All he saw was Sarah. The Sarah Bakker he'd left behind had matured, and she was breathtaking.

"Sarah." Levi pushed back his chair and was beside her in an instant.

Something heated inside Michael as Levi moved to the left and brought her into his line of sight. Her brown eyes grew wider until the whites showed all the way around. She stunned him again. One hand came up to cover her soft, pink lips. His heart sped up, and he braced himself for the sweating and fear that followed. There was none. Something around her neck caught his eye—a small sapphire on a silver chain. Was it the same one he'd given her? The hand about her mouth slid down and cradled the necklace, giving him the answer to his silent question.

"Michael?"

Chapter Seven

So this is how it felt to be frozen. A myriad of emotions bounced like a pinball machine inside Sarah. Michael, here, in front of her. Her Michael. No, he was never *her* Michael. That didn't matter now, and Aaron had some explaining to do.

"Sarah, are you all right?" Lucas asked.

His gentle hand rested on her shoulder and urged her to face him. She didn't want to. She'd lose sight of the most beautiful view she'd ever seen.

"Is it really him?" It was impossible. Had God finally heard her prayers?

Levi smiled. "Come on and say hello." Levi grabbed her hand and towed her away from Lucas toward a group of men she'd known her whole life.

Noah jumped to his feet, followed by Drew.

"Little Sarah Bakker, well, look at you," Drew said.

"Hi, Drew, good to see you." Her eyes wouldn't be moved lest he disappear again.

"Hi, Sarah." His voice was so soft. Rough. His tall stature was unchanged, although his usually tanned skin was sallow like he'd been without the sun for too long. The broad shoulders she'd often wanted to hang onto were slimmer than she remembered. His handsome face was so narrow, it looked carved from stone. And those blue eyes, usually filled with teasing and mischief, burned with soul-shattering pain. *Oh, Michael, what did they do to you?*

"H-h-hi," she whispered. Like two magnets pulled by an unstoppable force, Sarah flung her arms around Michael's shoulders and held on, unable to stop the flow of tears. For a long moment, she held him; and then with a sigh, his arms wrapped around her. "You're here," she said for only him to hear.

Michael stiffened and withdrew her arms from around his neck. Fire filled her cheeks. Whoops, her enthusiasm wasn't welcome. "S—s—sorry," she stammered.

"It's good to see you, too, Sarah," he said.

Something that made her pulse race filled his eyes. Was it . . . Michael blinked. Nothing. Just the same intense blue. Sarah mentally shook herself. Silly girl. Ignoring the urge to keep her attention on Michael, she glanced behind her. Lucas waited beside the restaurant host; she needed to get back to him. Torn, she took Michael's hand and waited until his eyes met hers again.

"I'm so glad you're back," she said. Michael nodded and smiled. "I'm glad to be back."

There was an edge to those words that she didn't understand. "I'll need that hand back," Michael said softly. Teasing her.

Blushing, Sarah let go. "I guess I better go."

Michael nodded. "I'll see you around."

Sarah waved to the brothers and made her way back to her date. Her pulse hammered through her veins, and her heart sang with joy.

"Wow, I haven't seen those guys since—Sarah, is everything okay."

"I think I overestimated my abilities today. I'm just a little tired. Nothing a good night's sleep won't cure."

"Do you still want to have dinner? We can leave if you prefer."

"No, I would love to have dinner. Is there anything you'd recommend?" Sarah asked.

Lucas smiled, appeased. She wasn't sure if the tension in her stomach was attraction or confusion. What a mess.

"I don't know; perhaps we should ask the waitress. This isn't my usual type of restaurant," Lucas said in a low voice. That only made Sarah feel worse.

"Can I tell you something? This isn't my kind of place either."

Lucas chuckled, clearly relieved.

"Someone told me this place has great food, and today is about new experiences. How about you order something, and I'll order something else, and we'll split."

"That sounds like a wonderful idea." Sarah relaxed back into her seat and sipped her tea. The buttery leather seat cradled her shoulders and back in its soft cushioning. Lucas retook her hand and gently ran his thumb over her knuckles. It was nice, warm, and comforting but only that.

A tall woman with blonde hair came to stand at their table. Her uniform was pressed to perfection. A name tag rested on the left side of her body.

"Good evening, sir and ma'am. My name is Kate, and I will be your server tonight. Are you ready to order?"

"Ah, yes," Lucas said. "What do you recommend?"

Kate rattled off a long sentence perfectly in Italian.

Sarah chuckled. "I'm sorry, Kate. I'm afraid neither of us knows what that is. Could you bring us two of your favorites, please?"

Kate smiled and graciously nodded. "You would be surprised how often that happens. I'll bring you the best in the house. Be back in a moment."

"She must think we're two country bumpkins out for a night on the town," Lucas said.

"Nah, I think she's as much of a hick as we are."

Sarah tucked thoughts of Michael's return into the back of her mind, but they refused to be silenced. Lucas deserved her full attention, and that was what she was going to give him.

Kate arrived shortly with a delicious marinara meatball dish and a flatbread pizza with smoked ham and cheese. Both smelled heavenly.

"So, Michael's back?" Lucas said.

"Yes, I can't believe it. After all this time. Mrs. Thomas must be thrilled."

"What about you?"

"I'm happy for his family and Aaron. Tell me about this new course you're presenting at the college."

The conversation took a safer route. The truth was Sarah wasn't sure how she felt about Michael's return. She was happy he was back with his family, and her brother had his best friend back; but for herself, that question was too complicated to answer.

When Lucas had eaten the last piece of pizza, he wiped his mouth. "Ah, Sarah, there certainly aren't any dull moments when it comes to you. I haven't laughed this much since forever."

"Neither have I; I think I've caught my second wind."

"Would you like dessert?"

"No, I am full to the brim. What about a walk by the lake before we end the night?"

"That sounds great. Let me just get the check, and then we can go." Lucas called Kate over. "Thank you so much; the food was delicious."

"I knew you would enjoy it."

Lucas paid the bill, and they collected their coats.

Light snow fell softly from the midnight blue sky; the moon glowed in the dark expanse. Bright lights twinkled from far-off buildings and became muted the closer they walked toward the edge of the water. Drawing Sarah closer, Lucas wrapped his arms around her and cuddled her. His embrace was lovely if she didn't overthink it.

"Thank you for tonight. I had a wonderful time with you. I had this idea of you from our school days, and now I discover the real Sarah is so much better."

She mattered. "What idea did you have? Was it bad?"

Lucas chuckled. "Far from it. Let's just say, I liked the Sarah I knew from school, but I like the one I'm getting to know much more." In a single movement, Lucas turned Sarah to face him. The darkness hid his eyes, but there was no mistaking his intent. She wasn't ready.

Unable to understand her uncertainty, Sarah stepped back and laid a gentle hand on his chest. "I think it's time to go."

Lucas smiled wryly. "Yes." He sighed loudly. "That's probably a good idea. Shall we?"

Lucas held out his hand, and Sarah placed hers in it. The gentleness in his eyes let Sarah know that he'd be patient. Smiling widely, she allowed Lucas to lead her to his car, and they began the drive back to her house.

"Can I pick you up for lunch tomorrow?" he asked as they parked outside her bungalow, admiring the stars.

"Yes. Can I meet you there? Mom is in the middle of an inventory count, and I promised I'd help."

"Sure. One o'clock?"

Sarah nodded. "Lucas, look. About earlier—"

"Sarah—"

"I do like you and—"

"Sarah . . . "

Hearing her name said with such tenderness stopped her ramble. "Yes."

"It's okay. I had a wonderful time tonight, and I hope we can have many more."

Sarah's heart fluttered. "Me, too. Good night, Lucas. Thank you for a lovely evening."

"Good night, Sarah."

She could feel him watching her all the way to the front door before he backed out of the driveway and drove away.

Her front door closed with a slap. Sarah shook the snow from her shoes and coat before she hung them on the rack. Purse in hand, Sarah walked up to her room and flung it onto her bed. A loud ping sounded as it crashed between her pillows. Oh, bother. Retrieving the purse from between her cushions, she swiped the phone open.

Lucas.

I look forward to seeing you tomorrow. Sleep tight.

Complete and utter mushiness.

Sarah snuggled deeper into her fleece blanket. Her novel rested on her bent knees. *Come on, Sarah.* She'd read the last page at least five times and still had no clue what was happening. Her thoughts kept drifting back to Michael. Seeing him again after all this time was like the day Nancy Adder had accidentally swung her field hockey stick into Sarah's stomach during gym class. The blow had winded her and left her dizzy and disoriented.

The book landed with a thud on the bedside table. Relaxing wasn't happening tonight. Exasperated, she threw herself out of bed and paced the rainbow carpet beside her bed. Michael. Memories played like a movie reel ending on their final night.

Sarah spotted a small, wooden box at the back of her closet between her shoes in the dim light. She hadn't touched it in three years. It held too many memories and foolish teenage girl dreams. Each page, picture, and item reminded her of Michael and the hopes she'd had for their future. With a light tap of her hand, the closet door drifted shut, and the box faded quietly into the darkness just as it should.

For a long moment, Sarah stared at the closed door before she lifted the book again and tried to concentrate on the words. Michael was her past, and for the sake of everyone, he would stay there. Another five minutes passed, another ten. Annoyed, Sarah slammed the bookmark into her book and flicked off the lights. Michael Thomas was alive. In the darkness, she let herself smile and thanked God that Michael was safe, home at last. Completely disregarding the wild thumping of her heart, Sarah snuggled deeper into her covers.

Chapter Eight

It's so quiet here. The rigid set of muscles in his upper neck and shoulders gradually eased as Michael turned onto Main Street. Snowy Springs hadn't changed much in his time away. The long road that ran along the town's central vein exploded with colors from the Christmas season. Garlands, with bright red bows, hung from every lamppost. Deep greens and red set off the delicate white snowflake lights and white snow. Large heaps of snow decorated the road on either side. The grocery store was more prominent than he remembered; the warm glow from inside reminded Michael of warm apple cider and pretzels available only during the Christmas season. Delmonte's Bakery, home of the town's best Christmas treats, was freshly painted. Outside stood an enormous Christmas tree trimmed in turquoise and silver. Probably Aaron's work. The familiar sight of Bob's Barbers, Lana's Bookshop, and Quick Cut Looks—the local salon—all decked in their best seasonal finery gave him a weird sense of nostalgia. With luck, Snowy Springs would be just what he needed.

Ambivalent, he brought the truck to a stop outside Aaron's store. *He'd be all right.* He'd repeated the exact phrase to himself and his family more and more as the time for his leaving grew closer. He was only a two-hour drive away; he'd come to visit on the weekends, etc., etc., etc. An expected wave of emotion choked him as he thought of his parents. He missed them already, but this was the only way he could see to keep them safe.

"You getting out?" Aaron's voice interrupted Michael's thoughts. He stood outside the truck with his beefy arms crossed over his impressive chest and the same cocky tilt of his head that Michael always remembered.

Michael grinned. "Right about the time you move out of the way," he teased.

Aaron chuckled and diligently stood back. Michael climbed out of the truck and stretched; his muscles twinged from the drive, and the scars on his back gave a familiar throb.

Out of habit, he did a sweep of the area surrounding him. All he saw was small-town life at its finest. There was no war in Snowy Springs.

"Wipe that grin off your ugly mug."

Aaron laughed, and the two embraced.

"Man, I can't tell you how good it is to see you. For the longest time, I thought you weren't coming back."

"Me, too."

"That bad, huh?"

"Worse."

Years faded. Aaron probably knew him better than his own brothers. "It's good to see you, man. I'm glad you decided to come." He clapped Michael on the shoulder. "Where are your bags? The apartment's all made up and ready to go. Avery and Sarah helped get the linen and stuff."

Michael tensed at the mention of Sarah's name and forced himself to relax. Being in Snowy Springs meant seeing Sarah. What he'd felt for her was in the past. He was too broken now for anyone. Reaching into the bed of the truck, Michael hauled out two duffel bags, all his belongings in the world, and heaved them onto his shoulder.

Aaron held out a hand, and Michael handed him one. "Follow me."

The screen door of the hardware store opened with a loud creak, and the bell above it jingled. It was warmer inside; the smell of wood, oil, and metal permeated the dim air. Michael followed Aaron to the back of the shop and up to the second level. His boots crunched over the dark hardwood floor as he climbed the stairs. The apartment opened to a small kitchenette-living room, with a breakfast nook included.

"Fridge's fully loaded; my sisters saw to it. If you need anything else, I'm sure you remember where the grocer is."

Michael grinned.

"Bathroom's across the hall," Aaron said and pointed to a door that stood slightly ajar. "Bedroom's that way." He opened the opposite door. A large bed with a blue comforter was featured prominently in the center of the room, and there was a small closet in the corner. One dark, square side table stood beside the bed, and on top was a white cylindrical lamp. It was clean and stark, and to Michael, it could've been a five-star hotel.

"Thanks, man. I appreciate you doing this for me."

"Yeah, well, I do have an ulterior motive for wanting you here. The Christmas program is less than three months away, and the community center's roof caved in last week. I desperately need another set of working hands. How much of high school co-op do you remember?"

"Quite a bit. Did a lot of building while on deployment."

Aaron seemed to understand because compassion filled his eyes. "If you need anything, let me know. I'm serious. Anything."

"Yes, sir." Michael saluted his friend and smiled. And this time, it almost felt genuine.

"Wise guy. Why don't you get settled in and then meet me at the bookstore? Mom's going nuts waiting to see you." Aaron rolled his eyes and let out a quick laugh. He dropped Michael's bag on the bed, already on his way toward the door.

"Thanks, man. Be down in five."

"You don't want to unpack?"

"Nah, I'll do that later." Aaron didn't need to know the horrors in his dreams.

In less than five minutes, Michael walked with Aaron from the hardware store and into the warm interior of Lana's bookstore. The sweet, citrusy smell of oranges mixed with coffee. And was that Lana's famous coffee cake?

"Michael." Lana rushed toward him, threw her arms around his waist, and hugged him tightly.

Lana was like a second mom to him, and all the trouble he and Aaron had gotten into in high school made Michael her biggest fan. Petite, dark-haired, and with a no-nonsense attitude, Lana Bakker was everything a good Dutch-born mother should be.

"Oh, my boy." She grabbed his face between her tiny hands, turning it this way, then that. "You need some fattening up." Where there was food, there was love. Lana lived by that motto.

"Relax, Mama. Give the man some space," Aaron teased and easily dodged as Lana took a swipe at him.

"Oh, hush, you."

Six-feet-seven, Aaron towered over his five-feet-three mom. Still, Michael knew there was nothing Aaron wouldn't do for his mom.

"Do I smell coffee cake?" Michael asked.

Lana beamed. "Yes, yes, come over to the kitchen. Sarah should have everything ready by now."

The three walked through the inventory boxes and to the small kitchen situated at the back of the bookstore. Michael paused and allowed Lana and Aaron ahead of him. He took a deep breath and crossed the threshold. Sarah was already there, her hair woven into a long braid. She wore a red turtleneck sweater and black slacks. Perfect for the cold weather. Her smile—the one that made his heart trip over—flashed as Aaron walked over and embraced his sister.

"What do you have for us, Squirt?"

"Aaron . . ." Sarah playfully swatted him. "I'm not a little girl anymore."

"I know, but you're still my squirt."

The coffee pot clattered back into place as Aaron scooped his sister into a hug. A twinge of something burned in Michael. *Leave it alone, Michael.* Any dream he had of him and Sarah had died in the desert sands. *But you're here, now, aren't you?* Yes, he was, but it no longer mattered.

Aaron released his sister, and Sarah's warm, brown eyes lifted to Michael's, and his heart thumped painfully.

"It's good to see you again, Michael. I wish my brother had told me you were back—you know, before the other night," she said softly and touched the chain around her neck. The one he'd given her. Her hands trembled.

Michael let the comment slide. "How have you been?"

"Good, you?"

"Good." Could she tell he was lying? Probably. Sarah had a knack for reading people; it was something that had made him nervous all those years ago. It was something that worried him now.

"Michael's decided to accept my offer," Aaron said and slipped his arm over Sarah's shoulder.

"Oh? Which one?"

"He's decided to put his co-op skills to good use and help me rebuild the community center's roof. And you get to boss us around," Aaron said with a comical frown. "Sarah's running the Christmas program this year."

"They still have that?" Michael asked.

"Yes." Sarah smiled. "And this year we're planning to sell some antiques from the historical society to build the Coopers a new barn. Theirs burned down during the fall—a powerline short."

Aaron added, "I offered to help rebuild, but between the high price of lumber and shortage of manpower, I can't afford to do it for free."

"Well, whichever way I can help, I'd be glad to." Anything to feel normal. To belong.

Sarah smiled again. "I'm sure they'd appreciate it."

"Then I guess we'll be seeing a lot of each other?" Why had he said that?

Sarah shifted, her delicate hands twitching. "I guess. It'll be good to work together. Be like old times, huh?"

Not if he could help it. There was almost nothing of the old Michael that remained. "I think your mom's waiting for us."

With his arm still around his sister, Aaron turned and followed Lana. *Forget it.* Michael scrubbed the back of his neck. He desperately wanted to feel normal, and here, with Aaron and Sarah, even more so.

Waiting for everyone to seat themselves, Michael sank into the chair beside Lana.

"So, Michael, how is your family?"

"Good." They would be better with him in Snowy Springs. Safer.

Lana nodded and dished cake onto four plates while Sarah poured four cups of coffee. He hid a smile as Sarah added chocolate to hers. He guessed some things never changed.

"So, where to now?" Michael asked Aaron after they'd said goodbye to Lana and Sarah.

"You don't want to take a day to settle in?"

"Honestly, I've been sitting on my butt for four months. I need to be busy; I need to do something."

Aaron nodded. "You want to tell me what happened to you over there?"

Michael shrugged. "I don't want to talk about it."

Aaron laid a hand on Michael's shoulder. "You're like a brother to me; I can see something is bothering you. And judging by the phone call I got from Noah two days ago, it's a lot worse than you're saying."

His brothers and their meddling. "I'm fine. Or now that I'm here, I will be."

"Fair enough. But if you need to talk, I'm here."

"Thanks, man."

"All right, onto the next thing." Aaron squeezed Michael's shoulder, smiling. "I'm going over to the community center and then to the Coopers' to take measurements if you wanna come along."

That sounded like a plan. "Great."

Chapter Nine

"I heard some interesting news this morning at the diner." Juliet slid her arm into Sarah's and pulled her away from a stack of books to be shelved.

Two cups of Snow Town coffee rested on the front counter of the bookstore. The vanilla latte smelled heavenly. Sighing, she put the stack in her arms down and turned to Juliet. It didn't take a genius to figure out what she'd heard. Within ten minutes of Aaron and Michael walking out the door of her mother's store, they'd received at least fifteen phone calls to ask if they knew Michael Thomas was back in town.

"You're not gonna ask?"

Sarah shrugged; this was not a conversation she wanted to have with Juliet right now. Not with the lingering pain in Michael's blue eyes burned into her memory along with the rough growl of his husky voice. And she didn't want to think about how tangled her emotions about that particular man were.

"Sarah, the boy you had a crush on for our whole high school career is back in town." Juliet stopped, stared at Sarah, her eyes narrowed.

"You knew," she said. What could Sarah do? There was no point denying it.

Here we go. "Yes, Lucas and I saw him last week in Denver."

"And you failed to mention this because . . ."

"Because it's not a big deal. Okay, maybe it's a bit of a big deal, but it's not in the grander scheme of things. Yes, Michael is alive, and yes, he's back in town. Case closed."

"Me thinks the lady doth protest too much."

"Knock it off, Juliet. Spare me your Shakespeare dramatics. That's old news; we both know it."

"Is it?" she pressed.

"Yes, it is. My feelings for Michael are in the past. Besides, I'm with Lucas now."

"Oh, do tell me about you and Mr. Hunky. Has he kissed you yet?"

"What? Are we in high school?"

"No, but why are you so evasive?" Why, indeed. Juliet crossed her arms over her chest, her foot tapping with impatience.

Today wasn't Sarah's day. Exasperated, she said, "Can we please talk about something else? Anything else?" Anything but her growing confusion.

Juliet regarded her, those green eyes cool, calm, assessing. "Okay, seeing that I'm such a generous friend, I'll let you off this time."

"Thank you. Now, what was the real reason you came to the store?"

"Callen and I wanted to know if you and Lucas would like to come to the rodeo with us next week. Ben Thomas is riding, and I'm dying to see Susie." Michael's youngest brother, Ben, was married to Juliet's sister, Susie. They'd given everyone a headache with their stubbornness. It had taken a valiant effort from Juliet and Levi to get them to admit their feelings for each other.

"I'll send him a text and let you know. If you don't mind, I have work to do."

"Sarah, what's the matter?" Her stern tone turned soft with compassion. Juliet knew her too well.

"I'll tell you when I've figured it out." Her voice rasped out of her chest, stemming from the heaviness resting there.

Juliet wrapped her arms around Sarah. "If you need a sounding board . . ."

"Thank you, my friend." She hugged Juliet back and then turned and picked up the stack of books. She swallowed hard, fighting back a wave of emotion. God had blessed her with a friend like Juliet. They'd been through so much together since their dollhouse days in first grade.

"Let me know about the rodeo, okay?"

"Sure. I'll text you as soon as I've heard from Lucas."

As abruptly as she had come into the shop, Juliet left, a blast of cold air following in her wake. Sarah took a deep, calming breath and sipped her latte. "Thanks, my friend," she whispered to the now-empty store.

There was a steady flow of customers as the sun traveled across the sky.

When night had fallen and the last customer had left, Sarah busied herself restocking the shelves. It was busywork that didn't require too much brainpower, and Sarah could work through her tangled thoughts.

When they'd received the call from his parents that Michael was M.I.A, Sarah had done her best to keep strong and support Aaron and her mother, while inside, she'd been slowly breaking apart. There'd been nights where she'd cried herself to sleep and prayed fervently for his safe return. As the years went on, those prayers had become fewer as her hope dwindled. But when she'd seen him that night in Denver, her long-buried feelings had surged to life.

"Stop it, Sarah," she whispered; if she took that road, it would only lead to pain again as it always had. Nothing had changed between her and Michael. He was still Aaron's best friend, and she was just Aaron's little sister. Besides, she was with Lucas now, and he didn't seem to mind her at all.

Laughing at her silliness, Sarah shot a text to Lucas and set down her phone to continue shelving.

It was well past dinner by the time Sarah locked up the bookstore. The stock seemed to be flying off the shelves quicker than she could replenish it, which meant many late nights. The chilly winter air bit at her nose and ears. She vigorously rubbed her hands together.

"Really." She gave the key another tug. The stubborn lock wouldn't budge. When would her mother get tired of it and call someone to fix it? Then again, lately, Sarah spent more time at the store than her mom. Her mom's arthritis flared up in the winter.

"Do you need some help with that?" a familiar male voice asked from behind her.

Sarah startled and spun around. "Michael, you scared me half to death."

Michael chuckled. "Eye's up, Captain. You never know what will be creeping up on unsuspecting beauties at this late hour." He was teasing; she could tell by the twinkle in his eyes. "Can I try?"

"This lock—I've been telling Mom for months we need it replaced, but . . . Anyway, yes, please, I would love some help."

Sarah stepped back and gratefully sank her hands into her coat pockets and allowed Michael to inspect the lock.

"Just needs some oil," he said, straightening. "Why don't you go into the hardware store and wait there? I'll get some oil and lock up."

"Are you sure?" She blushed at Michael's raised eyebrow. "Thank you."

Michael shrugged. "No big deal at all. What would Aaron say?"

Sarah could guess. She dropped her eyes and then noticed his running gear.

"What are you doing outside dressed like that? You'll catch your death," she said.

Michael flinched. "I'm tougher than that."

Her heart ached. "Yes. I meant it's freezing."

"Nothing I can't handle." He shrugged and shifted. "What are you doing here so late?"

"Inventory. The store is so busy during the day, I don't get the time to do it."

The cold wind gusted between them and then blasted them in an icy mist. Sarah shivered. She'd been outside wrestling with the door for longer than she'd thought, and she was freezing. The light snow that had begun to fall at midday had gradually turned into a raging blizzard without her noticing it, and harsh gusts of dense snow and wind hammered against her and pressed the cold deep into her bones.

Michael's eyes swept over her, assessing. "Come on, Sarah," he said. His voice was harsh, almost as if he was worried about something. He probably didn't want to see her tonight.

"I'll be fine. My car is just around the corner."

"Look, I may have been away from Snowy Springs for a few years, but I still remember the damage a snowstorm can do. You can't drive in this. It'll bury the car in three seconds. We can wait out the storm in the apartment."

Just great. Michael was in town one day, and already, the relationship of the hero and damsel in need of rescue had resumed. The stubborn set of his jaw and the fear in his eyes gave Sarah pause. There was no use arguing; it wouldn't do anyone any good. "Okay."

Michael took her hand and led her into the hardware store. "Stay here. I'll take care of the door and be right back."

Rolling her shoulders, Sarah climbed the stairs to the apartment. The wind howled outside, and thick clumps of snow pelted the windows. She shrugged off her coat and laid it on the back of the sofa, sinking gratefully into its softness. A smell she remembered from long ago drifted to her nose, and she inhaled deeply. Oh, how she'd missed that smell. It was Michael, pure and simple.

The hardware store door clattered, opened and closed, the lock sliding home. Michael jogged up the stairs. As he reached the landing, he shook the snow from his hair.

"Wow, it's coming down out there."

"Did the oil work?" she asked.

"Yeah, but I think Aaron should look at it. Coffee?"

"Yes, please."

A few minutes later, he handed her a steaming cup and motioned to the small settee beside a compact fireplace.

"Not a lot of room in here. Why don't we just sit here?"

Sarah sipped her coffee. It was warm and wonderful, the heat from the mug seeping into her cold fingers. Another loud gust of wind whimpered outside, and large puffs of snow splashed across the windows. Michael continued to sip his drink. The silence stretched just as it had in the bookstore. The past pinged like a pinball between them.

"I thought you were dead," she finally said.

Michael paused and placed his mug on the counter, seemingly gathering his thoughts. A shudder passed through his large frame. His hands clenched so hard, his knuckles went white.

"It was close a time or two. There were days I wondered how I made it through." His voice was low and rough, barely a whisper.

"Was it really so bad?" She reached out and found his arm as if she could help the agony emanating from him in some way.

Michael shuddered again, lost in what looked like an unpleasant memory. After a long silence, he nodded.

The ache in Sarah's chest intensified. "I'm sorry." There was so much else she wanted to say but couldn't find the right words. Michael had suffered, while she'd selfishly pouted about the fact that he wasn't home and didn't love her. At the same time, she'd fought day in and day out to forget him. A tear slid down her cheek.

"Don't cry," he said. "I'm okay."

Michael sighed, his hand gently patting hers. Tingles of warmth spread from his fingers and settled somewhere low in her stomach. It was an old feeling and yet a new one. Michael's touch had always had that effect, but it seemed sharper after such a long time, like a spark instead of a steady current.

Sarah smiled and removed her hand from under his. "I'm glad you came back."

Those blue eyes darkened and delved into hers. "I'll just . . . " Michael pushed himself up from the table, picked up their empty mugs, and took them with him. "I think we need to see what we can make for dinner." He grinned. "Mac and cheese?"

Sarah laughed. "Maybe you should let me handle that. I've eaten your mac and cheese many times. You know mine is better."

Michael smiled. The expression softened the haunted planes of his face. "Okay, point taken. How about I find the ingredients while you get the pasta going?"

"You're on."

Chapter Ten

"Soldier?" a brisk voice said in a heavy Pashto accent. "Soldier, wake up!" He didn't move, just let his head hang down to his chest. There was little point. He'd learned any response would bring a thrashing, and no response did the same.

The blows came again, punctuated by raucous laughter and jeering remarks. None of it made sense to him; their scornful expressions told him all he needed to know. These people hated him and everything he stood for, and for that, they punished him.

He came out of the dream screaming. Gasping for air, Michael bolted up from the spongelike bed beneath him. The blue comforter lay in a rumpled mess at the base of the bed. Sweat poured from his body. His heart raced as he clawed his way out back to reality. A nightmare. It was just a nightmare. He squeezed his eyes closed, inhaling and exhaling deeply, and reminded himself where he was. Gradually, his heart rate slowed as the cold night air bit into his bare skin. He shivered and climbed out of bed. He stumbled a few steps before coming to a stand—time for a shower.

Recollections lingered as the hot water sluiced over him, and he watched as it swirled down the drain, pumping his aching fists. If only it were that simple for him to rid himself of the memories. There would be no more sleep tonight. Now, he guessed, was a good time to unpack. Two dusty duffel bags thudded onto the messy bed. He zipped the first open to find a leather-covered book on top with a note attached. Chuckling, Michael sat down and opened the letter. It was from Levi.

Dear Michael,

As your brother, I love you, and I know that I cannot understand the horrors you suffered in your years away. War is a terrible animal, and it takes the heart of even the kindest man and turns it into dust. I know you've questioned God in that horrible time; and I know in times of deep stress and anguish, you thought God wasn't there. Believe me when I say, He was. God stood beside you each and every day. He wept when you wept and hurt when you hurt. The Bible says in Romans 8:38-39, "For I am convinced that neither death nor life, neither angels nor demons, neither the present nor the future, nor any powers, neither height nor depth, nor anything else in all creation, will be able to separate us from the love of God that is in Christ Jesus our Lord."

He is with you, and His love for you is unchanged.

Take care, my brother. I pray each day that you will find peace.

Levi

Michael wiped a lone tear from his clean-shaven cheek, surprised to see it there. He couldn't remember the last time he'd cried. During his time in the desert, he'd promised himself his captors would never see him cry. His one act of defiance to remain stoic and unmoved.

He set the letter on the bedside table and picked up the leather-bound book. It was as familiar to him as his own skin. Levi had given him this Bible on his first deployment. The thin pages crackled as he turned them over. Verses, highlighted or underlined, and notes littered the cream and black sheets, dates and memories attached to each one. Faith had been something dear to him, something he would have staked his life on until that night. He closed the book and tossed it onto the bed. After that night, everything had changed.

Morning inched across the sky as he lay in bed, the bright, glorious notion of a new day falling beam by beam across his shadowed face. Was Levi right? Had God walked through the pain and anguish with him? Then why had he felt so alone in those dark hours? No answers came—a fool's faith.

Unable to stay still any longer, he dragged himself up, ignoring his protesting muscles. It was time for coffee.

Michael slid a green sweater over his beige Henley that hung over his belted jeans. Where had he put his boots? He found them beside his bed and went in search of coffee. The small kitchen smelled of cheese and another scent he remembered distinctly. He smiled. In the hours it took for the storm to die down, he and Sarah had talked and laughed while she caught him up. In the times her eyes sparkled with laughter or her slender fingers swept her dark brown hair behind her ears, he would wish. He had no time for wishes; reality always knocked.

Massaging the tight muscles at the back of his neck, Michael flicked on the coffee machine, eager to get the day on the go. Aaron said he would be at the shop around nine; he glanced at the clock—barely seven.

He took his coffee cup with him into the downstairs workshop. The rich smell of sawdust and wood reminded Michael of high school and better times. Stacks of rough lumber lay heaped high against the shed's wall in preparation for the community center job. Aaron hadn't been kidding when he'd said he needed more human resources. Michael picked up the first piece and carefully checked the plans laid out against the wall; he might as well start somewhere. He lay the lumber between the guard and saw and got to work.

Two hours later, Aaron found him covered in fine layers of sawdust, pleased with what he'd accomplished.

"I would say I'm surprised to see you up so early, but honestly . . . " Aaron laughed and clapped him on the shoulder. "At this rate, we'll have the community center roof done in no time." He admired the neatly stacked planks.

Michael shrugged. "It felt good to do something. Sitting on my hands was pretty boring."

"Anytime, man, anytime." Aaron walked over and picked up Michael's mug. "Let's have a cup and discuss what to do today."

A cloud of sawdust trailed Michael as he left the workshop.

"I hope you don't mind me barging in like this. Your coffee was the first thing I smelled when I walked through the door."

"No worries. There's more than enough."

Aaron refilled Michael's mug, took one from the cupboard, and poured his own. "How are you settling in?"

"As well as can be expected, I guess."

"Not sleeping?" Aaron tilted his head and raised his eyebrow.

"Not much. The nightmares . . . " How to explain? "The nightmares are still pretty bad. I'd hoped that being here again would help, but . . . "

"No change." It was a statement, not a question.

Michael shook his head.

"Mike, give yourself time to heal."

"Let's hope time is enough." Aaron wouldn't understand his desperation to be normal.

Sensing the discussion was over, Aaron said, "During the building assessment done last week, we found out the roof has water damage in over eighty percent of it. It must've been from a leak years ago. In short, the whole thing needs an overhaul—struts, rafters, ceilings, everything. So, if you're ready, we can get going now."

"Who's going to handle the shop?"

"I hired a lady named Dakota. She looks after things while I'm out on the job. She should be in—" The bell on the front door of the shop jingled. "—Right now."

A strange smile lit up Aaron's face. Michael grinned. It seemed Aaron had a thing for his new employee.

"You gonna tell me?" he asked and grinned at his friend.

Aaron flushed. "Soon."

It took almost two hours for Michael to control the impulse to hide when someone pounded a nail with enthusiasm. He cursed as his hammer slid from his grip again and bounced onto the nearby floor. Thank goodness the ground was the only thing below him this time. One of the crew hadn't been so lucky earlier. He really hated this. He felt like a wimp.

"Wow, you're making good progress," Sarah said. A cloud of something warm and citrusy overpowered his senses as she stood beside him. A din of hammers smacking wood, voices, and wood saws filled the community center.

"Yeah, Aaron's got some good guys working for him. I'm just here to hammer in the nails." He carefully returned his hammer to his belt loop and rolled the stiff muscles of his shoulders.

Constructed from an old barn, the Snowy Springs community center had seven rooms branched off the main meeting area. Each year, the annual Christmas market was held in the central space. In contrast, the smaller rooms acted as stations for everything from cookie decorating to garland-making.

"What are you doing here?"

"Oh." Color warmed Sarah's cheeks. "Mom sent me. You know she constantly worries and most of the time for nothing. She has this idea that you two big, strapping boys would forget to feed yourselves. Her words, not mine."

He liked that this older Sarah had a little bit of spunk. Growing up, she'd been painfully shy around him. When she'd turned fifteen, she'd seemed to come into herself; since then, they'd become good friends. He chuckled at the look of utter horror faked in her expression.

"I think she just wanted to make sure yesterday wasn't a figment of her imagination."

"That would make sense. My mom did the same for the first week I was home. I didn't have any privacy, even in the john. I think she thought if she let me out of her sight, I would disappear again. My being away was very hard on her, on them."

A small hand gripped his arm. "Including you. It was hard on all of us." Michael wasn't sure he was supposed to hear her quiet words. She moved closer. His heart sped up in response to her closeness.

"Sarah?" someone called.

Sarah quickly stepped away from him with an unsteady smile.

"Lucas, what are you doing here?" she asked. The man pulled her closer and hugged her. Thank goodness he hadn't kissed her. *Leave off, Michael; she doesn't belong to you.*

"Your mother said you were working on something for the Christmas fair. I thought I'd take you to lunch."

Michael bristled. Lucas Williams. A growl built in his chest as Lucas wrapped his arm around Sarah's slim waist.

"Well, Michael Thomas. It's good to see you again." Lucas stepped toward him, his hand extended. "Thank you for your service." He grasped Michael's hand in his. "The whole town was so glad to hear you were back."

"Thank you." The words tasted bitter on his lips. What was he supposed to say? Thank you that the heroic dream he'd had of serving his country had turned out to be dreams built on ash and betrayal. And all for what? Nothing. Torture and the loss of the woman he loved. Just the idea of Sarah being with someone else burned like acid in his gut. "If you'll excuse me. Sarah, thank you for the lunch."

Sarah's smile dimmed. Michael felt terrible. *Deal with it, soldier.* The sooner he got used to seeing Sarah with other men, the better.

"Well, I guess we'd better go, then. Michael, please tell Aaron there's a basket inside his truck for you two. I'll see you later." Sarah tugged on Lucas' arm, and the two of them disappeared into the bright sunlight.

Aaron appeared at his shoulder, whistling. "Wanna tell me why you're scowling at my sister and her boyfriend?"

"No."

Aaron's grin grew. "If you say so. But I remember a Christmas . . ."

"How did you know about that?"

"A brother always knows," Aaron said cryptically. "I'm starving; let's go see what Mom sent."

Michael could do nothing else but follow.

Chapter Eleven

Sarah twisted and untwisted her fingers as she sat across from Lucas at Sue Ellen's Diner. The place was alive with voices and laughter; fifties music clashed with the raucous hubbub. Bright red chairs, orange booths, and blue tables artfully arranged around the room were like something out of a movie set. Along the walls in black and white, encased in grayscale colors, were Elvis, Marilyn Monroe, and Dean Martin's memorable faces. Sarah took another bite of her chicken sandwich and swallowed. What was that look on Michael's face as she'd walked away?

"Sarah, did you hear me?" Lucas laid a hand over hers, his green eyes burning with concern.

"I'm sorry, what?"

"I asked if we're still on for this weekend, snowmobiling?"

Sarah racked her brain. "Ah yes, sure. That sounds like a great idea. Where are we going?"

"There's a place in Leadville called Open Country Snowmobile that looks good."

"Sure, whatever you think is best."

Lucas turned her hand over and entwined their fingers. "Sarah, are you . . . I mean, you've seemed a little preoccupied over the last few days. Is everything okay?"

"I'm fine. I've just been so busy with the store and the community center. Mom is spending less and less time at the bookstore, and all day-to-day responsibilities rest on me. The roof falling at the community center has put a wrench in the Christmas program plans. Thank goodness, Pastor Ted is allowing us to use the church building for rehearsal, or who knows where we'd be."

Sarah closed her eyes and inhaled deeply. Lucas was right about her preoccupation but not only for the reasons she gave him. Michael was constantly on her mind. Last night had been a mistake; it had made the young girl in her want things—things she could never have with Michael. Yet here she sat with a man who clearly wanted those things with her, and . . . She was confused.

"Where, indeed. Is there anything I can do to help?"

"Aaron and his crew have everything under control, I think. It's just busy."

"If you're sure. I don't mind lending a hand. I mean, I spent a load of time climbing roofs on the ranch growing up."

"You know what, I'm going to mention that to Aaron; he might need another hand." Her phone buzzed beside her again, and she glanced down at it. "I have to get back. Mom is meeting the ladies' committee at the church to talk about pies for the Christmas program, and I have to hold down the fort."

Lucas sighed softly. "Remember, you promised Juliet the rodeo next weekend?"

"Yes, of course. Thank you for lunch." She accepted Lucas' hug before hurrying into the cold weather outside.

Laughter and voices greeted Sarah as she entered the shop. Sarah could hear her mother's low alto from the kitchen, and that deep baritone was one she knew all too well. Hanging her coat on the rack, she strolled to the back of the store. Sure enough, her mother and Michael sat together around the small table in the bookstore kitchen, coffee and her mom's vanilla cake spread out before them.

"Sarah, look who stopped by," her mother said.

"Michael, what a surprise." If sarcasm had a name, it would be Sarah.

Michael's eyes widened, and laughter filled the room. "I don't know, Lana. She doesn't seem quite so shy anymore."

So, she'd been the topic of conversation, then. Wary, she leaned with a shoulder against the door frame.

Her mother's laughter joined with Michael's—at her expense, of course. However, it lifted Sarah's heart to see her mother laugh with such obvious pleasure. Her mother hadn't laughed much since her father had passed two years ago.

"Don't you have work to do?" she asked, annoyed with the way Michael had managed to upend her life in the short time he'd been back.

"Yes, your brother sent me home. Something about being a danger around power tools."

His blue eyes met hers, filled with some dark emotion she couldn't name. There was something hidden there. But as he'd said, he didn't want to talk about it. She stepped more fully into the kitchen from her perch at the door. She'd seen it last night, too, when a question she'd asked or comment she'd made was a little too close to the mark. Would he tell her if she asked?

"So, you came to mooch cake off my mom instead?"

"No, actually, I asked Michael to help me with some shelving in the store." Her mother replied. "You and I have been talking about making the children's section bigger for the last few months. I thought if Michael was available to help, we might be able to make the changes before the Christmas season."

"Mom, I'm sure we could just ask Aaron."

"I did, and he sent Michael."

Okay, so she wasn't winning this round. "Well, when you're finished, the shelves are in the storeroom. Help yourself." Sarah spun on her heel and stormed off to the front counter, furiously stacking the books once she got there.

"You want to tell me why you're so mean to that boy?" her mother asked a few minutes later.

"Mama . . ."

"Don't you *Mama* me, Sarah. What's with you? It would help if you were glad that he's alive and here. Isn't that what you prayed for, night after night when I held you weeping in my arms?"

"Yes, Mama, it is. But now, there's Lucas, and I'm confused." How could she explain how ecstatic she was that Michael was back but also so terrified of what it might do to her heart?

Her mother's stern expression softened. "My Sarah, you have a bigger heart than anyone I have ever met, save for your father. There is room for Lucas and Michael. Lucas is a good man; he makes you laugh, and he will make a good husband. I know you have a complicated history with Michael, but that is all in the past. God has given him back to us, and as torn and broken as he is, he needs our love and friendship."

"Yes, Mama." Her mother tugged her closer and hugged her.

"It is the past, right?" her mother asked softly.

"Yes, of course." Sarah's breath caught in her chest as a shadow moved behind the shelves. Michael entered the room and stopped Sarah from speaking further.

Her mother smiled at them and let Sarah free from her hug. "Come, I will show you where the shelves are. Sarah, a new load of young adult fiction arrived while you were out; it needs to be unpacked."

Muttering to herself, Sarah got to work.

The afternoon moved quickly. Michael hung shelves, and Sarah unpacked books in companionable silence. Then Mama announced that she would be leaving, complaining her joints were aching.

"Do you want me to drive you home and get you some soup?" Sarah asked.

"No, no, I'm having dinner with Avery and the kids. I might spend the night in the guest room there."

"Okay. Bye, Mama. I love you."

Mama hugged her tightly again. "I love you, too. Both my children," she said and hugged Michael before leaving.

"That's the last one." Michael stretched his long arms above his head with a loud groan. Thick scars peeked out from below the line of his dark green Henley.

Sarah stifled a gasp. Her heart broke all over again for his suffering. *Oh, Michael.* "Getting old?" she teased, determined not to show her seesawing emotions. Michael didn't deserve her wrath. After all, her expectations were never his, only hers and hers alone.

Michael stiffened, lowered his arms, and turned to her. "Are you talking to me?" he asked and pointed to his chest. "Because I thought you were mad at me for some reason."

"I wasn't mad. I just . . ." Maybe if she came clean about her high school crush on him, all this would be easier. "It's just that in high school . . . " Oh, this was so embarrassing. "Never mind. Anyway, thank you for your help today. You've saved me hours of nagging Aaron to get this done."

Michael nodded. "Not a problem; kept me busy."

"I'm sure you know how much this will mean to my mom. I mean, with my dad gone and . . . "

"Are you going to tell me what she was talking about earlier?"

A vice grabbed her around the neck. *Keep it calm and cool, Sarah.*

"Just something better left in the past, that's all." Sarah shrugged. She hoped he wouldn't ask any more questions she couldn't answer. Well, not *couldn't*, just preferred not to.

"Are you sure? Because I'm sure I heard . . . " His expression tensed; Sarah's stomach dropped. Had he guessed how she felt? "Best left in the past, right?" He went to the supply closet to fetch the broom. "I guess I better clean this up," he said. His voice was oddly formal like he was trying to put some kind of distance between them. But why?

Michael swept while Sarah went around the bookstore and closed the windows and blinds in preparation for going home. The store slipped into darkness, save for the light burning outside on the signboard. "Are you ready to go?" she asked.

Michael nodded, his hands on his hips. "Can I ask you something?"

"That depends." Was he going to ask about earlier again?

"Why Lucas Williams?"

"Why not? Do you have a problem with me dating Lucas?" Maybe her voice was a bit sharp.

Michael raised his eyebrow. "You know he's the reason Aaron and I spent half of senior year as slaves for Mr. Smith?" His expression was severe, although the laughter in his eyes gave him away.

Sarah laughed. "Oh, come on, Michael. That was ten years ago; surely, you're over that. After all, you and Aaron did deserve it." She sobered as Michael's face darkened. So that's how it was? "Besides, I don't think it's really any of your business who I date, is it?" The question was a challenge, and she could see by the hardening of Michael's expression, it had hit the mark.

A moment of tense silence passed. He shrugged, his face haggard. "No, I guess not."

Awareness thickened the air around them. Sarah's hand clasped the necklace, an old habit. Michael's eyes followed her movement and widened.

"I still don't know why you gave this to me. It was way too much for a Christmas present," she said, silently asking him the question. In an almost unconscious move, she reached for the clasp.

In an instant, Michael was inches away. His warm hands touched hers and brought them slowly back in between them before he let go and stepped away.

"That color always looked beautiful on you," he said softly as if he was far away somewhere.

Sarah needed to know. Maybe it was time to be more direct. "Why did you give this to me?"

Michael went rigid. "Why does it matter?"

"It matters to me." Could he understand what it had meant to her? Had it meant the same to him?

"It was a Christmas gift, nothing more." An arrogant mask she'd never seen dropped over his face. Something inside her shattered. Avoiding her, Michael bent down and picked up the tools and measures. "Do whatever you like with it."

A cold gust of wind blew into the shop he opened the door. "Good night, Sarah," he said. All harshness was gone from him. Only raw pain that welled with the ache inside her remained.

Stunned, Sarah swallowed hard. He wouldn't make her cry again. Not this time.

Chapter Twelve

S nowy Springs Full Gospel Church was well into the worship part of the service when Michael walked in. He'd come today because the idea of staying alone in his apartment for one more minute was slowly driving him crazy.

"I'm glad you made it," Aaron whispered. He moved to the next chair and gestured to the one where he'd been sitting.

"Yeah, yeah, running a bit late." He'd been up for hours. The nightmares had woken him, and he had gone hiking in the vast forests that surrounded their small town. Somehow, tramping through inches of snow and black wilderness didn't seem nearly as daunting as his empty apartment did. He'd climbed to the top of Great Ridge Hill and sat there until the sun rose. His Bible had somehow ended up in his backpack, along with his water bottle and snacks. He'd found it and opened it for the first time in years. Colorful, underlined verses came quickly to memory as he read them. He still wrestled with the truth he knew those words held and prayed for the faith to accept the power they had. It was part of the reason he'd decided to come this morning, despite his dislike for loud noises and crowds.

Lively music washed over him. The last time he'd been in a church, he still believed in a God of mercy. Now, his faith was floundering, and he was barely holding on. *Well, I'm here. Over to You, God.* Maybe he would give God the benefit of the doubt today.

As the music came to an end, a tall, dark-haired man got up to speak. He spoke simply and eloquently about faith and how faith is tested under pressure and in trials. Michael glanced up. What about war? The man spoke simply and sincerely, but Michael knew nothing was easy or straightforward about it.

The man ended with a final prayer, and Michael stood to leave. His heart was heavier than before. Over to his right, Sarah and Juliet, heads bent together, whispered furiously. Neither looked at him, but he somehow knew they were discussing him. Sarah wore a sleek, dark gray jersey dress with black leggings and boots. She was so beautiful.

The hardwood-backed pew pressed into Michael's hand as Lucas wrapped an arm around Sarah and drew her close. How was he going to do this? He knew he was no good for Sarah, but when . . . He blew out a deep breath. *Keep your head, Michael; she's with Lucas.* Now, if only he could convince his heart to let Sarah go.

"Something interesting over there?" Aaron asked with a huge smile

"No," he growled.

Aaron laughed. "You know, Mike, you can lie to yourself and me for only so long. If you want my advice, don't wait too long."

"Mind your own business. How are things with Dakota going?"

"Very well, thanks for asking." Michael wanted to smack the teasing grin off his buddy's face.

"Anyway, lunch is at Mom's place today. You're coming, right?"

"Yeah, yeah, I'd said I'd be there."

Lucas and Sarah walked hand in hand out the church doors, and hurt tore through him. It became unbearable as the thought of Sarah in a white dress with Lucas appeared in his mind. *Easy, man.* The chair creaked in protest under Michael's hand.

"Okay. Okay. Chill. I was only asking." Aaron chuckled as he backed away, his hand held out in surrender.

Michael rubbed his sore hand. Aaron wouldn't be smiling if he knew how close Michael was to losing it. What was going on with him? Michael shuffled out of the large, white building and tried to act as expected. Flashes of past memories invaded his thoughts and made it difficult to concentrate. And then there was Sarah. He'd never been so aware of someone in his life. Perhaps the safest place for him was to be alone, but then he would have only the nightmares to keep him company.

Emotions under control, Michael pulled up outside Lana Bakker's house. Sunday lunch was an occasion that often brought the two families together. That was when his parents still lived in Snowy Springs. It looked the same as he remembered. Long, white pillars braced the gray, triangular roof, and the second story divided into two triangular eves. Sarah's room had been to the right. He could remember the times he'd glance up and see Sarah. When he'd caught her gaze, she'd blush and disappear. He wished he knew why.

Shrubs and bushes formed a barrier around the cozy front of the wrap-around porch. He had many good memories of this house. In his mind's eye, he and Aaron chased each other over that green lawn, laughing as they unloaded their water pistols. And Sarah, young and shy, watched the action with her book a safe distance away. He stood a long time, remembering, reliving, and wishing he could forget what would come years later.

"Michael?" Lana called and waved from the open door. "It's much warmer inside, and there's cocoa."

"How can I refuse an offer like that?" He forced a smile. Lana didn't need to suffer his lousy mood or numbness.

The house opened like a time capsule. Memories assaulted him in such quick succession, he had to stop for a moment to catch up. The last time he'd been inside this house was the night he'd been about to tell Sarah he loved her. The mistletoe hung in the exact place it had then. He could almost imagine Sarah, with her citrusy scent, so close to him.

Swallowing hard, he shook himself out of the daydream. That was a different life. He was another person now, splintered by war and guilt. Blackness rolled over his eyes, and he fought it back. He would carry his guilt and pain like a soldier because that was what he was.

"Michael, are you all right?" Her sweet voice called him back from the grave. Sarah.

"Y-y-yeah." He cleared his throat. "Yeah, I'm okay."

With soft eyes filled with compassion, Sarah watched him. The care in them was unmistakable. Without a word of explanation, she led him to a small sitting room at the back of the house. He remembered it as Sarah's father's office; it wasn't anymore. He sat heavily into a single-seater couch. Sarah took a seat opposite him.

"Are you okay?" she asked softly.

Michael swallowed back his irrational anger. "Yes, no, I don't know." It was too easy to be honest with Sarah. "Do you care?" he asked.

The words came out harsher than he intended, and Sarah gasped. Color ebbed and flowed into her cheeks, and she drew a deep breath. "We've been friends our whole lives. It hurts everyone to see you like this."

"You, too?" Why had he said that? But as messed up as he was, he wanted to know.

The sapphire pendant twisted between Sarah's fingers. "Yes, me, too. How can we help?"

The sincerity in her words cut him to the quick. Guilt gnawed in his gut along with the fear that choked him. "No one can help me," he rasped.

Sarah rose from her seat and kneeled before him. Her hands rested on the armrests with his, her sweet face inches from his. "You're wrong."

Attraction pumped through his veins, and he forgot about impossibility. Sarah waited. Hands on his, lips within his reach.

"Sarah, you don't understand," he whispered. How could he tell her just how much his captivity had cost him? Her lips pressed together, and the thought of kissing her swept over him.

"Help me, then. I want to help." She pushed to her feet and gave him room, as if sensing the danger. "Whenever you're ready, we'll be here."

Michael nodded, unable to speak. His heart rioted inside him and roared past the warnings of his head.

"Michael?"

"Huh?"

"I asked if you wanted to go snowtubing tomorrow." Her eyes danced with amusement. At him, no doubt.

He grinned at his foolishness. "Don't you have work?"

"No, tomorrow is my day off. We're heading to the slopes for skiing and tubing. Will you come?" Sarah rubbed her hands together. Her face shone with excitement. Who was this Sarah?

"I thought you hated any activity in the snow. As I recall, you can't even ski."

"People change, you know." Whoever this feisty Sarah was, he kinda liked it.

"Who's we?"

"Me, Lucas, Juliet, and Callen. Oh, Aaron said he might come if he can swing it."

Lucas. Great. Just what he needed.

"A miracle would've had to happen for you to do anything that didn't involve a book."

"It did."

"Oh?"

"Yeah, you came home." With cheeks as red as the sunrise, Sarah turned to leave the room. "You coming?" she invited.

Michael was by her side in two long strides. For her, anywhere. "Yeah, I'll come."

Sarah smiled softly. "I'm glad."

"Sarah, why are you hogging Michael? His cocoa is getting cold," Lana called from the kitchen.

"I think we're about done. Eight a.m., okay? Don't keep me waiting." She sashayed into the kitchen. Michael couldn't help but smile. This woman.

"What are you smiling about, Michael Thomas?" Lana asked and looped her arm through his.

The kitchen smelled delicious and looked the same as it did in his memory. The wide refrigerator stood between the pantry and stove. Gray marble counters lined the room above light, wooden cupboards. The back door, closed now, usually hung open in the summer while Lana baked. The cool afternoon breeze brought with it the smell of jasmine flowers. Today, a pot roast in the oven, a loaf of fresh bread on the cutting board, and garden-fresh vegetables—a feast for a king.

"Nothing. Sarah is different than I remember her."

Lana raised an eyebrow. "Grief will do that to a person."

"Lana?"

"Our girl really struggled when you didn't come back. It's good you did."

Another mystery. Michael didn't ask what she meant, afraid he already knew.

"Help me set the table." Lana handed him plates and cutlery. "Sarah should have the table ready for you."

He narrowly missed Avery's two little ones squealing as Aaron chased them through the house. Their harassed mother following close by.

"Hi, Michael," she said.

"Avery."

"You're looking . . . well, alive." He and Avery didn't get on; he never did figure out why she didn't like him.

"And kicking."

"Well, I . . . " She disappeared out of the room, presumably in search of Aaron and the kids.

Michael crossed to the dining room. His thoughts were full of Sarah and what Lana had said.

"Mom put you on duty today. Aaron is such a cheater; he always gets out of chores," Avery said with mock annoyance.

"His chore is harder, I think. He's running after the young ones. I can't believe how big they are. Piper was just a newborn when I saw her last, and Wyatt was barely out of diapers."

"Three years is a long time," she said. She sounded sad.

"Tell me about it. It's like coming back from a time-warp. When I left, things were a certain way. Nothing much changed for me while I was in the desert, and now that I'm here, everything has changed. People changed, and I feel like I've been left behind." Words he hadn't had the guts to admit to himself spilled out in a flood.

The salt and pepper shakers clattered onto the table as Sarah crashed into him. Her gentle arms wrapped him and hugged him hard. He held her and ignored the voice that told him she belonged to Lucas. For that moment, he enveloped her and held on.

"I'm sorry," she whispered. Her head fit perfectly into his shoulder like it was made only for her. Maybe it had been. Michael squeezed his eyes shut and then opened them again. He hoped he could control the tempest inside him by some long shot of the imagination. He loved this woman, and she could never know.

"Me, too."

Chapter Thirteen

The horn blared as she laid her hand flat on it. Where was that man? Just then, Michael turned up the street toward her, his hands held out in apology. Dressed in running gear and a heavy-looking black backpack on his back, Michael looked like he hadn't slept at all. Worry fizzled through her.

"You look like something the cat dragged in. When was the last time you had any sleep?"

"Not all of us can look as fine as you first thing in the morning." Mischief twinkled in his eyes, and he smiled. After their encounters at her mom's house yesterday, Sarah hadn't known which Michael she would find this morning. Her friend or the brooding soldier.

"This takes hard work, you know," she teased. Michael didn't need to know she'd gotten little-to-no sleep last night, too. "Lucas and the others are waiting for us at Echo Mountain. We can lag for an hour if you'd like to get some sleep?"

"Nah, I should be okay. I didn't go too far this morning, but I could use a shower." He smiled apologetically.

"Okay." She followed Michael into the apartment. "I'll make some coffee."

"I'd be grateful."

Sarah busied herself around the kitchen; she'd lived in the apartment before she bought her house, and all the cupboards opened with practiced memory under her hands. She smiled when she found a small box of peppermint kisses in white and silver sparkly packaging. Michael had always loved them. She'd bought them for him every Christmas and even sent some to him when he was deployed. They smelled heavenly. *Focus, Sarah; make the coffee.* Unable to find the container, she went in search of Michael. The bathroom door was still closed.

She knocked. "Michael?"

"Yeah." The door swung open.

"Where's the . . ." Her sentence died at the sight of Michael's bare chest before her. Heat flooded her cheeks.

"Sorry, where's the coffee?" she asked breathlessly.

"Oh, sorry, in the bottom of the fridge."

"Thank you." Sarah grabbed the door handle to pull it closed. A glimpse of his line-raised back reflected in the mirror behind caught her eye. "Michael, what happened to you?" she asked. The words came out before she could caution them.

Michael's expression shuttered. "Can we have this discussion after I've showered?"

She nodded, and he closed the door. *Oh, Michael.* What had he suffered over there?

Coffee mugs clattered in her shaking hands as she filled them. One for her and one for Michael. How had Michael gotten those scars? Probably with something sharp. She felt sick at the thought. The rich aroma of fresh coffee filled the room and stilled her racing heart. Inhaling the smell, she took her first sip. Delicious.

Fully clothed, Michael returned to the kitchen. Some of the exhaustion was gone, but the dark rings under his eyes seemed to be permanently etched into his face. To her, he was still as good-looking as ever with the heart to match. He always had been, and therein lay the problem.

Michael picked up the coffee and took a deep swallow. "You're a lifesaver, you know. I still don't know how you do it, but you always make the best coffee. Believe me."

Sarah laughed. "I highly doubt it. I happen to have it on good authority that Avery's coffee is much better than mine."

"Aaron?"

She nodded.

"Aaron wouldn't know a good cup of coffee if someone nailed it to his forehead." They laughed together. All the Bakkers knew Aaron's penchant for strong, black coffee.

"Are you ready?"

Michael yawned and stretched. "Yeah, let me just get my stuff."

Sarah swallowed. "About the scars . . . " Michael's mug trembled as he placed it on the counter. The barstool beside him creaked as he landed in it. "You don't have to tell me," she whispered.

He shook his head. "It's okay. Before I say anything, how much did my parents tell your mom when they found me?"

"Not much. Only that you were in Germany and would be home soon. They said you were injured. That's about it. I spoke to Aaron after that night in the restaurant, but he said the same."

Weariness stole over Michael's face as he stared down at his mug. "I was tortured. Every day, an officer would pull us out one by one from our cells." He paused, swallowing hard. "After we were trussed up like pigs, they'd whip us. I can't remember how many; I always passed out after twenty." He clenched his trembling hands tighter together.

Something inside Sarah broke. A soft cry escaped her, and she found herself wrapped around him again. Wetness ran down her face as strong arms held her close and gently ran a hand down her back.

"Don't cry, Sarah. It's okay. I'm okay."

How could he say that? He wasn't okay. He was hurt and in pain; she saw it each time she looked at him.

"Don't lie to me, Michael," she said. "You are not okay. Even I can see that."

As soft as butterflies' wings, something brushed her forehead. "I would never lie to you, Sarah." His voice was low, fervent, like a promise. He may not be lying, but he wasn't saying everything either.

Disentangling herself, she straightened her shoulders and cleared her throat. "So, are we going?" she asked.

"Sarah . . ." Seeing her resolve, Michael rubbed his hand down his face and mumbled, "Yeah, I'll meet you in the car."

The main road opened to the freeway and headed to Echo Mountain. Michael sat beside her and frowned; tension hung like a cloud in the car.

"Michael?" she asked. They'd crossed an invisible line earlier, one that could end only in disaster.

"Michael?" she asked again.

"Yeah."

"Are we okay?"

He blew out a long breath. "Yeah, can we just forget about earlier? I'm not saying keep what I told you a secret. I'm just not ready for my mom to know yet."

"Okay." She wanted to ask why; but Michael had his reasons, and she would respect them.

"How are things with the Christmas program going?"

The Christmas program. This, Sarah could handle. "Pastor Ted and the elders have arranged for more of the churchmen to help with community center renovations. The stage, four of the rooms, and backstage should be ready for the market and the pageant."

"So, what happened? Aaron told me the roof caved in from a huge snowstorm last winter."

"Well, we thought the damage from the snowstorm wasn't so bad. What we didn't see were the number of small cracks made by the weight of the snow. We had heavy rain in the spring; the roof leaked everywhere. When the ice came, the whole roof collapsed in on itself. The rooms in the back were filled with snow. Not to mention the damp, which made a huge mess. So now, all rooms need to be re-roofed, and the floors re-laid. I'm not sure we'll make it in time."

Michael's hand covered hers. "It'll be all right."

She smiled. When he looked at her like that, she believed it would be.

"Why don't you try to get some sleep? I'll wake you when we're close."

Michael leaned his head back on the headrest and closed his eyes. "Thanks, Sarah. For everything."

A lone tear rolled down her face, and she wiped it. Was it possible for a heart to break with compassion? He didn't let go of her hand.

Did someone ever get used to the beauty of this place? Echo mountain stood high and proud in its snow-covered magnificence. The late winter spruce and pine trees speared the open blue sky. Small, white clouds drifted on the breeze. The weather was perfect.

Sarah parked the car beside a red jeep with *Juliet* as bold as brass on the vanity plate. Beside the jeep was Aaron's black truck and, of course, Lucas' gray SUV. Further down the path the lodge stood picturesque in the face of its crisp, tree-cluttered background. Sarah sighed as she looked up to the ski lifts that floated in timed slowness to their hills' destinations. A short, sleek run ran from the front of the lodge and disappeared into the trees below. People in blue tubes screamed with glee as they slid past. Excitement bubbled through her.

"And here we are," Sarah said as she gently shook Michael awake. He stretched and yawned loudly, and Sarah was pleased to see he looked more rested than before.

"Are you sure you want to do this?" Michael sounded serious, but as she glanced at him, his mouth ticked up.

"Me? Who hasn't been skiing for a while?" she teased.

"At least, I've been more than once in my life," he retorted, laughing.

Sarah took a deep breath of clean, mountain air. The day was beautiful. It was made more beautiful by the fact that Michael was beside her.

"I'm serious. Are you okay to do this?" he asked.

"Ah, didn't know you cared so much," she teased.

Her heart stuttered at Michael's soulful look.

"I care, Sarah." Of course, he cared. As Aaron's best friend and her unwanted substitute brother.

Together, they climbed out of the car.

"Where have you been?" Juliet asked, followed quickly by Aaron, Callen, and Lucas.

Sarah shifted uncomfortably. There was no way Lucas could have missed how close they were standing. Sarah straightened her spine; she had done nothing wrong. Then why did it feel like she had?

"We would've been here sooner if Mr. Slowpoke here could remember where he'd put his gloves." Sarah gestured flippantly to Michael.

He laughed and shrugged. "What can I say? It's been a while." Michael snorted.

One by one, they began to laugh.

"Okay, who's ready to ski?" Juliet asked. Her overwhelming enthusiasm was contagious.

"Not me. I agreed to come today because someone told me snowtubing was fun," Sarah said with a raised eyebrow in Aaron's direction. He shrugged and whistled lightly to no one in particular.

Juliet clapped loudly. "Skiers with me, the rest with Aaron."

Mouth open, Aaron gaped at her. "Juliet . . . " Sarah shot him a pleading look. "Fine, tubing it is."

Sarah sighed, relieved, but the surprises kept on coming.

"I'm with Aaron," Michael said.

Lucas frowned. "I'm with Aaron, too." There was no mistaking the challenge as his eyes grazed Michael. Oh no, he had noticed, and he wasn't too happy about it.

"Can I talk to you for a moment?" she asked. Lucas nodded and followed her.

"Hi," she said, accepting his quick hug.

"Sarah, before you say anything . . . "

She silenced him with her hand. "Lucas, I know you love to ski, and I don't want you to miss out because of me. Go with Juliet and Callen. I'll go a few rounds with Aaron and meet you back at the lodge." She purposely didn't mention Michael's name.

Lucas shifted and cleared his throat. "Do I have something to be worried about with you and Michael? You seemed awfully close."

"Nothing is going on, Lucas. He's just a friend. Go. I'll see you later."

"Are you sure?" he asked.

"Yeah, hopefully those lugheads won't be too much trouble."

"Okay, thanks." Lucas threw his skies onto his shoulder with a quick kiss on her cheek and ran to catch Juliet and Callen.

"So, where do we get the tubes?" she asked as she returned to where Aaron and Michael were waiting.

Aaron and Michael stood side by side, disapproval on their faces. Great, they were doubling-teaming her. She'd hated it as a teen and despised it now.

"Want to tell me why that boy was kissing you?" Aaron asked.

"Which boy?" she asked, playing dumb.

"You and what's-his-name," Michael chimed in beside him.

They were just ridiculous. "You both know I'm an adult, right?"

Both men crossed their arms over their impressive chests, unmoved. She'd had enough.

"Really?" Nothing. "I'm going to have fun, and when you two killjoys are done being preposterous, feel free to join me," she said as she stormed off. Who in the world did those two think they were? Her parents?

Sarah was almost at the head of the line when Aaron and Michael joined her. "You can't just walk off like that. Who knows what trouble you'll find?" Aaron asked.

"What's gotten into you? I start dating someone, and you turn into the Incredible Hulk."

"That's because he's your first boyfriend. I'm doing the big brother thing; it's like a code."

Michael nodded, his expression somewhat incredulous.

"And what's your excuse?" she asked. "The code, too?"

A red flush filled Michael's cheeks before his expression hardened. "No, it's you, and that makes it my business."

What was happening here? Did she care what Michael thought about her dating Lucas? He had no right telling her whom she could and couldn't date, just like her brother.

"First of all, what happens in my love life is absolutely *none* of your business. And second of all, I'm going now. I've had enough of this absurd conversation."

"She must be really mad; she's using big book words," Aaron whispered loudly to Michael. They both laughed but thankfully didn't follow.

It was her turn to go. Sarah grabbed the nearest tube and threw caution to the wind. She landed with awkward bounces before sliding unchecked down the icy run. The wind brushed her chilled cheeks, prying her from her dark mood. This was awesome. By the time she'd reached the end, adrenaline fired through her. She had to go again. Grabbing her tub, she lifted it and trekked back up to the start to wait her turn. Out of nowhere, two strong arms grabbed her from behind.

"What in the . . . "

"I'm sorry," Aaron said. "I had no right. For all the years, it was Michael, and you were safe. And now . . . "

"You knew?"

He sighed and nodded. "I worry, Squirt. That's all. I don't want to see you get hurt."

Sarah threw her arms around her brother. "You're forgiven. Give Lucas the benefit of the doubt. I know you and Michael didn't like him back then . . . "

"With good reason!"

"That was ten years ago."

"Still, it was the whole spring break."

"Oh, for goodness' sake. Lucas . . . " Sarah pressed her lips together as loud bellows of laughter filled the air.

Aaron was just about catatonic beside her. "I'm teasing, Squirt."

"You better be."

"Did I miss something?" Michael asked. His clear, blue eyes were focused like a laser beam on her, causing the mutinous ants in her stomach to riot.

"I think I'll just . . . " Aaron said and disappeared into the crowds.

"No, I was just trying to convince Aaron to give Lucas a chance, despite what happened in high school."

"Any luck with that?" he asked.

"Not as much as I would like."

"Are you ready to forgive me?" Michael laid a warm hand on her arm and gently turned her to face him. "I'm sorry, and you're right. I have no business interfering in your love life."

Appeased, Sarah nodded. The truth was he did have a say, and that was very, very bad. "You're forgiven."

"Are you ready to go again?" she asked.

"More than you could know," he replied softly.

Chapter Fourteen

This was one for the record books. Michael dodged the heap of bodies in amusement. Sarah lay on the snow beside his feet, gasping with laughter as she struggled to get up. Their third run down the tube slope had ended in a tangle when Aaron's tube collided with Sarah's and brought them in a bundle to his feet.

"Oh no, you don't," Aaron said and pulled Sarah down once again.

Michael felt something soften inside him. What would it be like if he could live life in the moment? Where there were no haunted memories, only joy. Where Sarah laughed with such luster, bright and filled with happiness? His heart skipped painfully. What would this day look like if he'd been honest with Sarah that night? He shuddered. Maybe it was Providence he hadn't.

Aaron pushed to his feet and pulled Sarah up with him. "You wanna go again?" he asked.

"I don't know. Sarah?"

"Yeah?" She dusted the snow from her seat and hands.

"Are you ready to try those slopes now?" Aaron asked.

"I think I might give it another go. On one condition . . ."

"What's that?" Aaron asked.

"Neither of you interfere."

"Interfere?" Aaron smiled innocently.

"Yes, for all I know, you two will get some silly notion, and I'll end up crashing into something," she said, hands balanced on her hips.

Michael's happy mood sobered as he remembered the times they'd pulled pranks on Sarah and Avery. The innocence of those times was lost to him, and he would never get it back.

"Okay, I promise. Michael?"

"I can't promise that I won't be the one to cause the interference. It's been a while."

They returned their tubes and headed back to the lodge to rent skis and poles. Aaron disappeared to check availability while Sarah and Michael waited outside. It was something to be out in the mountains; it felt so good to be in the open again. It teemed with life all around them; sounds, sights, and smells bombarded his senses. He closed his eyes as the sensations overwhelmed him. *Focus, Michael.* Breath by breath, he picked out each one and felt it, smelled it, and tasted it—the cold snow in his gloves, the bright sun in its blue haven in the sky, the smell of pine needles, and the sound of laughter. And the sweet citrus of Sarah beside him.

"You seem far away," Sarah said.

"Just getting perspective."

"What kind of perspective?"

"On life. What life was, and what it is now. You know, the easy stuff."

A peal of tinkling laughter filled the air. "Right, the easy stuff."

Michael pushed the door open and allowed Sarah to walk ahead of him. The smell of cocoa and the din of voices greeted them inside.

Aaron turned from the reception desk and met them. "The others aren't in there. They're probably still on the slopes."

"Right, so it's just us then?" Michael said.

"Looks like it," Aaron replied.

"Are we trying the green run?" Sarah nodded to the large ski map above them.

"I think I might head to the blue. Michael?"

"I think maybe I'm going to try the green first and work my way up to the blue."

"You sure? It hasn't been that long," Aaron said. They collected their equipment and headed back out.

"It's been long enough," he said bitterly. He and Aaron had been skiing since they were old enough to walk. Still, the trauma he'd experienced didn't care about history.

"It's okay, Aaron. I'll make sure he doesn't hurt himself," Sarah said.

"Michael, maybe you'd better come with me. It's safer," Aaron said. "With her, you might get some permanent damage."

"Hey. Just because I haven't spent my life out here doesn't mean I'm terrible," Sarah said.

Aaron's shoulders shook. "Yes, but . . . "

"It's okay. Seriously, I just need to find my feet again. I'll catch up with you later, okay?"

"Okay, but don't blame me if you end up in the hospital." Aaron clicked his boots into place and waited in line for the ski lift.

Moving carefully, Michael clicked on his skies and bent to help Sarah with hers.

"So, exactly how many times have you done this?" he asked.

The gentle swish of ski against snow sounded as they moved in tandem to the incline.

"Time to come clean. I went skiing for the first time three weeks ago. You know me." She shrugged.

He did. "And yet, here you are."

They stopped at the top of the run, and Michael's palms became slick with sweat. Maybe this hadn't been such a great idea. Perhaps he would just wait for the others back at the lodge.

Sarah smiled and grabbed his hand, squeezing it as if sensing his unease. "You ready?" she asked softly.

That smile had the power to undo him. And unsurprisingly, the knot in his stomach dissolved.

He nodded. With Sarah beside him, he could face anything. Pushing aside the whispers that remained, Michael moved closer to the slope. Young and old flew past them. Sarah grinned, excitement dancing in her eyes. Another hard thud beat in his chest. He smiled back and moved into position.

"Are *you* ready?" he asked, lining up his skis beside her.

"I think so; it's just . . . " Sarah wobbled, lost her balance, and crashed into him.

"Easy." She was so close to him that he could feel the mild exhale of her breath on his cheek. If he inched forward, he could . . . With a quick turn of his body, Michael planted Sarah back on her feet and moved away roughly, clearing this throat.

"You good?"

"Yes, thank you."

Before he did something stupid, he propelled himself down the slope. From deep in his chest bellowed the sound of freedom. Muscle memory took over, and his body moved and bent like it was second nature to him. It was like flying again. A smear of green and white and all the colors of the rainbow flew past him. His adrenaline soared. For the first time, the oppressive fear and anxiety he'd carried with him lifted, and light flowed in. Blood beat through his veins; warmth filled his limbs; and life bled back into him. For the moment, the voices were silent. Michael turned in triumph to see where Sarah was. A wave of fresh powder blew over him from Sarah's skis as she stopped.

"So, what do you think?" she asked. A red glow of exhilaration beamed off her cheeks. It was beautiful.

"That was amazing. I forgot how much fun this was. And bonus, I didn't fall on my face."

Sarah chuckled. "You didn't happen to speak to Juliet today, did you?"

"No, why?"

"Because that's exactly what happened to me."

"You up for another round?" Adrenaline beat through him. He had to go again.

"No, I'm going to grab some hot chocolate and rest these muscles. They're going to need some serious Epsom salts again." She groaned.

Chuckling, Michael climbed onto the next lift for the green run. As he rose up, the promise of freedom called to him, demanding him to answer. And answer he would.

After a few hours on the slopes, Michael trudged back to the lodge, exhausted and stiff but happier than he'd felt since coming home. After returning his equipment, he unzipped his jacket. He was about to throw it on a nearby sofa when Aaron rushed up to him, followed by Lucas.

"Is Sarah with you?" he asked urgently.

"No, she came back here over an hour ago, said she was going to have hot chocolate and wait for the rest of you to get back. Why?"

"She isn't here," Lucas said.

"Did someone try her phone or ask at the reception desk?" Michael asked.

"Juliet is there. We're waiting for her to come back and let us know. I think her phone must still be in the car." Right where they'd left it before hitting the slopes. Where was Sarah? Was she hurt? Anxiety writhed inside him like a spitting cobra.

In an instant, Juliet was back with them. "The lady at the desk says she saw Sarah a couple of hours ago. Apparently, Sarah grabbed a map from the main reception and said she was going for a walk."

"Did she say which direction she went?" Michael asked.

"No, but she did see someone who looked like Sarah heading toward Great Ridge Peak."

"Then that's the way we should go. Michael and I will head toward the ridge. Juliet, you and Callen wait here in case she comes back. And, Aaron, you go to Whitetail run; it runs parallel with Great Ridge."

A day that had started so perfectly was slowly fading into one of the worst days of his life.

"You ready?" Lucas asked and handed Michael a torch and flares he'd acquired from the lodge.

He nodded solemnly. "I'm not sure if we can get a signal out this far, so keep one of these on you as well."

Lucas handed him a satellite phone. Michael checked the frequency, and when he was satisfied it worked, he followed Lucas. The dying sunlight descended behind the trees and turned the hiking paths into trails of danger. Where was Sarah? Why was she out here alone? Sarah and the outdoors had never been friends.

"Are you a praying man, Michael?" Lucas asked as they walked.

"I used to be."

"What changed?"

Michael hesitated. "A lot of things."

"Fair enough. You know I was always jealous of you in high school."

"Why? You had nothing to be jealous of."

"You don't know, do you?" Lucas asked, his expression shadowed by night.

"What are you talking about?"

Lucas cleared his throat and continued walking, leaving his question unanswered. Something whispered in his memory. The conversation between Sarah and Lana at the bookstore. Had it been about him?

Lucas stopped, flashlight focused on the ground. "There are two sets of prints here. I'll take the left; you take the right."

"Okay. And, Lucas, if you pray, now would be a good time."

Lucas nodded in understanding. If they didn't find Sarah soon, it might be too late.

Using the flashlight to guide his way, Michael stared off into the distance and then moved as quickly as was safe down the trail's right side. The snow began to fall again, and the temperatures sank further below zero. Michael rubbed his gloved hands together and gripped the flashlight tighter. Sarah had to be okay; she had to be.

The dying sun gave way to the light of the moon and the inky darkness. Michael walked on, straining his senses to hear anything—a whisper or whimper or the sound of footsteps. Something to tell him where Sarah was. He continued on. The atrophied and punished muscles in his body ached from tension, the old wounds stiff from the cold. There wasn't a chance he would stop searching, even if he fell down dead. He would die looking for her—his last act of love.

Hours dragged by, and still, there was no sign of Sarah. The forest grew thicker around him; the trail of footsteps had long ago disappeared. Michael pressed on and on. Exhausted and his strength fading quicker than the retreating night, Michael leaned against a tall oak tree. Breath gasped out of him; hopelessness thrashed in his gut. Where was Sarah?

God, if You're out there, please help me find her.

A rustle of leaves caught his attention. He listened harder. Another rustle, followed by a small moan.

"Sarah?" he called. Hope pumped strength into his weary body, spurring him forward. Another whimper, this one sounding more painful than the last.

Michael moved forward using all the skills he'd learned while in the service. The bright beam of his flashlight cut into the darkness between the trees, and he caught a hint of something red. Sarah's jacket was red. Cautiously, he moved closer until the light pooled around the prone form of a human body. It was laying deadly still.

"Sarah?" He rushed closer. Sarah lay curled in a tight ball, her right leg stretched out. Michael pulled off his gloves and laid a finger against Sarah's neck. Relief filled him as her pulse beat softly against it. She was alive, but hypothermia would soon kick in. Michael touched the outstretched leg, and Sarah moaned. She must have hurt it. He needed to get her out of the cold and fast. Holding her close to him, he flipped open the satellite phone and dialed Lucas.

"Come on, Sarah; stay with me. Please don't leave me. Not like this."

The call connected. "Lucas, I found her."

Chapter Fifteen

Loud howls broke the silence of the night. Michael froze and moved to protect Sarah. Coyotes weren't an uncommon occurrence in the forests of Echo Mountain. The howling moved closer to the spot where he and Sarah waited. White eyes glowed in the searchlight as Michael swiveled around. They needed to move—and fast. Tenderly, he lifted Sarah into his arms, the flashlight clutched awkwardly under her shoulders and his other arm cradling her knees.

"Hang in there, Sarah." He kissed her forehead, inhaling the sweet scent of her skin, and followed the rough path he'd made back toward the lodge.

Adrenaline pushed his tired body forward as he stomped through the diminishing darkness, his beloved cradled against him. The howling came closer, the pounding of the pack running in tandem growing louder. Michael broke into a jog. It was slow and unsteady but moved him on. Still, the coyotes came.

Conceding that he couldn't outrun the group, Michael made a decision. He stuffed the sliver of fear away. There was only one thing to do. Face them.

"I'll be right back," Michael said and lay Sarah against the trunk of an old oak tree beside the path. Kissing her again on the forehead, he clutched the flashlight tighter.

A small branch in one hand, the flashlight in the other, Michael made himself big and bellowed loudly. He slammed the two together with a loud crash. For a moment, the howling stopped, and the steady thump of paws paused. He shouted and brought the flashlight and branch together again. An eerie silence filled the forest. Michael waited, breathing heavily. A loud yip, followed by intermittent howls, signaled the retreat.

Michael sighed and brought down his arms, collapsing to his knees. They would make it out of the forest. He pushed himself to standing using the torch to as a prop.

His tired body protested vehemently as he picked Sarah up again and walked steadily back toward the path. The pastel dawn broke over the mountain peaks and lit the way. Exhaustion dragged at his limbs, and with sheer willpower, he walked on.

In the distance, he heard voices. He was almost there.

"Michael?" Aaron asked.

Lucas, Juliet, and Callen waited behind him, their expression ranging from relief to sadness. Michael stepped out of the forest onto the grounds of the ski lodge.

"Is she okay?" Aaron lay a gentle hand on his sister's forehead. Behind him, the local medical staff waited, ready to take Sarah to the nearest hospital.

"Yes, I think she has hypothermia."

"Here, let me take her," Lucas said. Michael reluctantly shifted Sarah into Lucas' arms, feeling the loss deeply. He should be the one with her. Swallowing a lump in his throat, he said, "Take care of her."

Lucas nodded. "Michael?" His eyes held the same deep emotion that Michael was sure boiled inside him. "Thank you."

"You're welcome." A deep sorrow had taken residence inside Michael. The truth stared back at him. He could never be with Sarah. She was Lucas' now. His care for her was unmistakable.

Deep lines curved across Lucas' pale face softened as he gazed at Sarah. "I'm going to take her from here." Lucas hurried over to the medical staff, who whisked Sarah into the ambulance. The doors closed, and they drove away.

Aaron watched them leave beside him. "Thanks, man. I owe you one. As it got darker, I wasn't sure we would ever find her."

A shiver raced up Michael's spine. It had been close, but . . . Michael squashed that train of thought. Sarah was going to be all right.

"I care about her, too." He could feel Aaron's eyes burning into him. He must've heard the raw emotion in Michael's words. There was nothing he could do to take it back.

"I think I'll just get out of here," Michael said.

"Do you mind driving Sarah's car back to town? I need to get to the hospital."

Michael shrugged. He didn't want to go to the hospital, didn't want to sit in the waiting room filled with Sarah's friends and pretend he was part of them, that he was there for any other reason than his selfishness. "Let me know if she's okay."

"You aren't coming?"

"Nah, let someone else be the hero tonight," he said.

Aaron nodded and handed over the keys. "Drive safe."

"You, too. See you in the morning?"

"Yeah, I'll see you at the workshop."

Michael stumbled back to the truck. His energy was gone, and his limbs hung heavily on his body, his abused muscles beginning to stiffen. His heart was the heaviest. The urge to follow the ambulance to the hospital almost overpowered him. But he held back. Sarah didn't need him; she had Aaron and Lucas. She wouldn't even miss him.

Inside the car, with an unsteady hand, he whipped off his hat and ran his fingers through his sweaty hair. Michael stared off into the distance, questions and regrets folding over each other. What if he'd never left? Would he be the one with Sarah in the ambulance and not Lucas? Would Sarah want him to be? The white hills colored by the soft glow of dawn held no answers. Maybe there were none to be had.

More frustrated than ever, Michael shifted into drive and headed back to Snowy Springs.

Who'd brought the thrash metal band? Groggily, Sarah opened her heavy eyes. She winced as she tried to lift her head. Pain blazed up her leg. Where was she? White surrounded her—walls, ceiling, and the covers over her bed. There weren't any windows in the room, and two other beds lay empty opposite her. Why was she in the hospital? The last thing she remembered was . . .

You've really done it this time, Sarah.

"Hey, easy there," someone whispered beside her. "You're in the hospital."

"Aaron?"

"Hey, Squirt, nice of you to join us." She groaned; she hated it when Aaron called her Squirt. He was apprehensive about her. "You gave us quite a scare. What were you thinking, wandering off on your own?"

Lucas nodded in agreement. There was something bitter in his expression. What weren't they telling her?

"I didn't go far," she rasped. She pressed a button, and the bed lifted her to sit. Lucas, bless his heart, handed her a cup of ice chips. "Thank you."

"If Michael hadn't found you—"

"Michael? Where's Michael? Is he also in the hospital?"

Beneath his relief, Lucas' expression darkened. Guilt swept over her. Perhaps her plea for Michael sounded too passionate. She met Aaron's questioning gaze before her eyes dropped to her hands. It had. The door opened. Sarah lifted her head as Juliet and her mom entered the room. They moved aside to allow Lucas to exit. Where was he going?

"Michael's on his way back to Snowy Springs with your car."

"Oh." That hurt. Feigning nonchalance, Sarah asked, "What happened to me, and why is my leg throbbing?"

"What do you remember?" Aaron responded.

Pushing aside the strangeness of Lucas' leaving and Michael's absence, she let her mind wander. A blur of sights and sounds ran through her memory. "I took the Great Ridge Path. The receptionist said if I just followed the path, it should take about thirty minutes to walk the trail. After an hour, I knew I was lost; I think I was heading in the wrong direction and missed the turn to take me back. I wandered for a long time. It was cold, and the light was fading. And that's all I remember."

Something elusive tickled her memory. It disappeared like air as soon as she focused on it.

"You don't remember hurting your leg?"

"No." All this was puzzling. Why did the pine smell mixed with a scent she remembered as Michael burn so bright in her memory? Aaron tipped the corner of the sheet up to her knee, and Sarah gasped. Dark blue and purple marks splattered her skin at the knee. The rest of her leg lay wrapped in a large, white bandage.

"You didn't break anything, but you sprained your leg pretty badly. The doc says you'll be off your feet for at least a week."

This couldn't be happening. She didn't have time for this now. "What? But the Christmas program and pageant . . . "

"We'll take care of it," Juliet and her mother said in unison, coming closer to the bed. Both looked reassured at Sarah's noticeable alertness.

Her mom wrapped Sarah in a hard hug. "I'm so thankful you're okay. I prayed so hard."

"Thank you, Mama. I love you."

"Sarah, if you weren't injured, I would rip you out of that bed and . . . " Juliet's expression crumbled. Fat tears rolled down her face as Sarah leaned forward and wrapped one arm around her friend.

"I'm okay," she said. "A little banged up. Good thing Michael was there today."

Lana and Juliet glanced at each other before both sets of eyes turned to her. She was so busted.

Juliet's hand landed on her leg. Sarah grimaced.

"What's the matter? Must I call a doctor?" Juliet asked.

"No, it's sore, but I think I can handle it," she said weakly, happy to have sidestepped their curiosity.

When everyone was satisfied she was going to live, the doctor chased them out. Sarah lay staring at the walls of her ward. Lucas hadn't returned, and deep in her heart, she knew why. She cared about

Lucas and would miss his company, but her heart still belonged to the man it always had. Michael was back, and although her heart waxed and waned between hope and screaming denial, that is where it would always remain.

In that moment, as if called by name, the door swung open, and Lucas stuck his head into the room.

"Is the coast clear?"

"Yes, of course, come in."

"I'm sorry I disappeared earlier, but I, uh . . . I thought you needed some space."

"Why would you think that?" Lucas shifted uneasily. "Lucas, is something wrong?"

"Sarah, I want you to be very honest with me. Do you still have feelings for Michael?"

"Ah." Sarah bowed her head over her hands, purposefully hiding her eyes from Lucas' inquisition. "I'm sorry," she whispered.

Lucas sighed loudly. "Me, too, Sarah. I . . . " Another long sigh. "I guess I should go."

Ashamed, Sarah didn't look up as he left the room. "Goodbye, Lucas," she whispered as the door closed.

Chapter Sixteen

He'd lost the battle. Michael's truck idled beneath him as he debated the wisdom of giving in to the impulse to make sure Sarah was okay. His phone rang. He let it go to voicemail. Probably one of his brothers again; they'd been tag-teaming him all day. It rang again. He sighed and lifted it to his ear.

"Hello?"

"Michael?" his father said.

"Hi, Dad." Guilt pressed his chest.

His father whispered something to someone and then said, "Son, h-how are you?"

How was he really? Heart pounding in his chest, regret laying on his shoulders like a heavy mantle, and the ache for Sarah beating against his better judgment, he replied, "Not so good."

There was silence on the other side before his mother's voice came on the line. "What can we do to help?"

Nothing. There was nothing they could do to help. But he said, "Just keep praying, Mom; just keep praying."

"We will. We love you."

"I love you, too."

Swallowing hard, he ended the call and pressed the phone into his forehead. He missed his parents, but somehow, someday he would make it up to them.

When the message of Sarah's discharge had come through from Aaron, he'd already been halfway out the door. The light in the living room was on, and he could see Sarah moving in stop-start motions from the kitchen into the living room. Where was Lucas? And why wasn't he there to keep an eye on her?

Michael rubbed his jaw. *Come on, Michael, fish or cut bait.* Lucas would probably be back soon. He'd send Sarah a message. As he shifted his truck into drive, his phone pinged in his pocket.

I know you're out there; you might as well come in.

Busted. Michael threw his coat over his shoulders and walked briskly to the door. The little sleep he'd managed to get the night before had been crowded by torturous thoughts of Sarah. Sarah lost in the wilderness. Sarah cold and stiff when he found her. Sarah dead in his arms. That dream circled his memory until no power on this earth could have kept him from seeing her. Pathetic.

"Come in," Sarah called when he knocked.

The doorknob cracked under his hand as he turned it, and he let himself in. "You know, you shouldn't leave your door unlocked like that. Who knows who could just walk into your house?"

Sarah snorted. "In Snowy Springs? We're not in Denver, Michael."

She was angry with him. Why? Because he didn't go with her to the hospital? That was Lucas' job, not his—as much as he wished it was.

He shrugged. "You never know."

Michael walked deeper into the small room. Sarah sat on a long, gray sofa, her injured leg propped on a footrest. Her book rested on the table beside her, along with a cup of strawberry tea—Sarah's favorite.

"Why didn't you stay?" she asked stiffly.

Michael sighed; he supposed the truth was best.

"You were okay and going to the hospital. Lucas and Aaron were there. What did you need me for? Where is he, anyway?" Aware of her hostility, Michael sat on the one-seater chair beside her sofa. He turned to face her.

"That's none of your business."

Her words surprised him. "Has he contacted you?"

"Why didn't you come to the hospital?"

Deciding Lucas was a topic best left alone, Michael returned to Sarah's question. "I don't like hospitals. They remind me of Germany."

It was the only truth she needed to know. She didn't need to know what it had done to him to watch Lucas carry her away. How it had ripped into him. "Aaron kept me in the loop."

"Oh," she said softly.

Distress emanated from her being. If Michael hadn't been watching her so closely, he would have missed it. Kneeling before her, Michael took her hand and sighed. Something inside him relaxed, like a taut wire that had suddenly been given slack. Sarah's hands stilled and opened beneath his and allowed him to weave his fingers into hers. Sweetness flowed from the touch of her skin.

Lifting one hand, he ran his finger along the slope of her neck and lifted her chin, so Sarah's eyes were forced to meet his. Her chocolate browns were soft and filled with fathomless thoughts he wished he could understand. Unable to pull back from the way she drew him, he traced the smooth skin from chin to crown and back. Sensations tingled through his fingers, pulsing warmth through his dry veins. Sarah's pulse raced beneath his fingers in time with his own.

"Sarah . . . " he said huskily.

She trembled, her breaths loud and unsteady. Michael moved closer and rested his forehead against hers as his arms slowly slid around her waist.

"Sarah," he whispered. The warmth of her skin burned him like the fire of the sun. There was no stopping it; there was nowhere to hide from it. Slowly, Michael closed the distance between them. The first soft brush of his lips against hers, his knees buckled.

"Wow," he breathed before moving in for another taste. Sarah tasted like joy, sunshine, and sweetness all rolled into one person. Her lips were soft as he tenderly kissed them. There would never be another woman for him, only Sarah. Reluctantly, he broke the kiss before his chaotic emotions overruled his head. He unwrapped his arms from around Sarah and moved back to his seat.

"Michael, why . . . " Sarah cleared her throat, her eyes wide with wonder. "I guess that wasn't too bad in the way of first kisses."

Michael just about fell off his chair at her declaration. "What?" he exclaimed.

Sarah's cheeks flooded with color, her hands twisted once again in her lap. "Oh, you know—"

A loud knock on the door interrupted her. The knock sounded again, only this time more impatient than the first.

"It's open," Sarah called.

Lucas came around the corner and immediately stopped in the doorway. His open expression transformed into something Michael knew well. Lucas was jealous.

"What are you doing here?" Lucas demanded.

Unwilling to put Sarah in an impossible situation, Michael stood to his feet. "I came to check on Sarah."

"Oh, okay. Well, I'll just . . . " Lucas made a move to leave.

"No, I better get going, anyway. Sarah, Lucas . . . goodnight."

It cost him to ignore the bewilderment in Sarah's expression, but he had to leave. Sarah was better off with Lucas, not him. He didn't look back until he was in the cab of his truck driving back to his apartment. He'd just made a huge mistake.

The harsh bite of the cold water hit his dry, cracked skin. The lashes burned like fire as they ran down his back. Michael gasped as unfeeling hands thrust him into a frozen, metal seat and tied his hands and feet with thick, clunky chains. Harsh voices shouted in the darkness, followed by heavy blows. His sore body blazed with pain at each new strike. The edges of his vision faded into blackness, a brief reprieve from the torment.

"Soldier?" a brisk voice said in a heavy Pashto accent. "Soldier, wake up!"

He didn't move, just let his head hang down to his chest. There was little point. He'd learned any response would only bring more blows. No answer would do the same. The blows came again, punctuated by raucous laughter and jeering remarks. None of it made sense to him; their scornful expressions told another story. Finally, his torturers tired of their sport and dragged his semi-conscious form back to the dank cell. The dingy cell was made up of little more than concrete; a thin, dirty blanket; and a bucket to complete his loss of humanity. Humiliation was the primary tool of the enemy, and they used it with vicious effectiveness.

"Thomas?" Sergeant James Martins said from the next cell. "You alive?"

"Barely." There was no part of him that didn't ache. Blood poured from his broken nose. Another of his teeth had been knocked loose. He'd be a sight if anyone could see him. The dim light didn't do much to break the

stifling darkness. His spirit had long since dwindled. He rested his head on the icy wall behind him; frigid concrete cooled the burning in his back. He shivered. The blanket wouldn't do much, but it was better than nothing.

Crawling over to the small cup of water at the cell entrance, he rinsed his mouth and tried to clean blood from his face. There was nothing he could do about the wounds on his back. Even now, trickles of blood ran down his ragged skin and formed a pool where he sat. The blanket would soon be soaked. He threw it over his shoulders, anyway.

Another scream rang out from somewhere in the darkness, a blood-curdling shriek that cut off abruptly. His brokenness split further from pain. No doubt another soldier had died a horrible, excruciating death. Silence followed, and then the stomp of boots came closer, the creak of the cell next door opening and closing. Michael squeezed his eyes closed as they dragged a pleading Martins away. Michael doubted he'd be coming back. One by one, his troop were being hauled away; desperate screams would follow; and then, an eerie silence. They weren't seen again.

The rattle of gunfire resounded in the darkness, followed by raised voices, some Pashto, some American. More shots sounded as the definitive sounds of death reached his ears. Michael waveringly pulled himself to his feet. He firmly gripped the bars in the small window of his cell, straining into the darkness. One thought rang in his mind. Freedom.

A tall, fully decked-out figure came to a stop at the door, his night-vision goggles swinging up and down as he appraised it. "Move back, soldier. I'm going to blow the lock."

Shaking knees buckled, and he stumbled back further into the cell. A loud bang chimed in time with the continued barrage. Michael shrank back as the shadow loomed over him.

"Don't worry, soldier, we're here to get you home."

Michael lurched up in bed, heart racing, his body slick with sweat. The sounds of battle still rang in his ears. He glanced at his phone—one a.m. and another missed call from his parents. He wiped his face with trembling hands, surprised to see wetness drip off his fingers. Guilt, sorrow, and gratitude wound together in a giant balloon that expanded into his throat and shut off his ragged sobs. Many men had lost their lives that night. Martins' body, along with others, had been retrieved and transported back to their families in the U.S.

Shivering, he reached for his shirt. He was one of the few who had made it home outside a body bag. Tears that he could no longer hold back spilled from his eyes and formed rivulets on his cheeks. *Oh, God, help me*, he whispered, desperation peppering each word. The very air around him seemed to congeal and form a barrier bearing down on him from every angle. He needed space and openness like he needed his next breath. He needed to get out of there.

Throwing on some clothes and shoes, Michael climbed into his truck, pointed the nose in a direction, and drove. He opened the windows wide and allowed the bitterly cold night air to fill the cabin, breathing it in deeply as he went. The Main Street of Snowy Springs was deadly quiet, as it should be in a small town at one a.m. The town's festive Christmas lights shone merrily. Colorful, glowing bulbs and happy decorations brightened the inky black night. The beauty and peace it represented slowly calmed the emotion roaring in his chest. He turned the corner and drove on.

Chapter Seventeen

Sarah groaned and flipped her pillow over again. She hoped the coolness on the other side would help alleviate her splitting headache. With a sigh, she lay down again. Her leg ached; her head hurt; and most of all, her heart . . . Well, it was just a gamut of emotions.

What had happened to Michael that evening? First, he'd kissed all good sense out of her and then left her to deal with Lucas. Chivalry was apparently a quality Lucas still possessed in spades. He'd brought her dinner. His offer of friendship had surprised her until she'd seen how genuine it was. *Urgh.* Men. Can't live with them, can't live without them.

Giving up sleep as a bad joke, Sarah tossed aside the covers and winced as her swollen foot came into contact with the cold floor. Perhaps another painkiller would at least help two of the pains. No medicine could help the one in her heart. The stairs creaked eerily as she gingerly walked to the kitchen and grabbed a glass and pills from the counter. Quickly swallowing down two, she sank onto the nearby sofa and relived the kiss in technicolor film.

The gentle and tender way Michael's lips had held hers made her toes curl. Her stomach fluttered. It was completeness, like two halves of the same whole meeting each other. It had been bliss right up until the moment where Michael clammed up and ran away.

What do You think, Lord? Am I setting myself up for heartache again? When it came to Michael, she couldn't trust her feelings; she was blind. Her heart overruled her head, common sense, and anything else possibly affected by emotion. All that was left was prayer and her Bible.

Sarah maneuvered back up the stairs and picked up the blue leather-bound book beside her night lamp. It held a treasure trove of memories, promises, and tears. Those painful murmurings that had stained the pages during Michael's absence had long since dried their words imprinted on her heart. She opened her Bible.

Be still before the LORD and wait patiently for him (Psalm 37:7).

At the time, she'd wondered what the verse meant. Was it that Michael would love her or that he would return? Nights of anguished prayers and questions flittered through her memory. As she remembered those prayers, it was clear that God had been speaking to her even then about Michael's return. Overcome once again with gratitude, Sarah slid down to her knees balancing most of her weight on one knee. Her heart ached for Michael, not only with love for him but also for the suffering and pain that blazed in those deep blue eyes. Bowing her head, she let the tears run. Only God could help Michael. She slipped back into bed and finally succumbed to sleep.

The light shone painfully behind her eyelids as Sarah awoke the following day. The little drummer boy had been joined by an entire symphony that throbbed through her whole body. And then there were the dreams—dark dreams of battle and blood. Michael pleading with her to run. Aaron shouting while he pulled her away from him. A coyote howling somewhere in the background. Her fall had impacted her mind more than she'd thought. Whatever it was, she was glad to be awake—or as much as her body would let her be. Pain shot up her leg as she straightened it and tried to stand. She ached in places she hadn't known she could.

A hot bath with her favorite bath bomb sounded like heaven. Shuffling, she readied the tub and smiled as the smell of lavender and mint rose with the steam. Sighing softly, the warm water covered her shoulders as she lay back and relaxed.

When the throbbing in her muscles eased and her headache was all but gone, Sarah got ready for the day ahead. Her peaceful morning was disrupted by the loud screeching of the doorbell. Who could possibly be here so early in the morning? The clock ticked the hour. Ten a.m. She was very, very late. The doorbell chimed again.

"Hold on, I'm coming," she muttered, wincing as her swollen leg bumped against the newel post of the stairs.

Surprise skittered up her spine as the door swung open. Standing in the bright morning light was a very sheepish-looking Michael.

"I come bearing pastries," he said and held out a white, square box. How was it that with haggard black smudges under his eyes, Michael looked good enough to take her breath away? He stepped closer just as another car pulled into the drive. Aaron. Michael glanced over at the car and then at her. With a quick smile, he handed her the box of pastries and hurried back to his truck. So much for that.

Aaron shook his head as he watched him go before turning around with another bakery package in his hands.

"It seems I'm beaten." He threw an arm around her shoulder. "How are you feeling?"

"Sore," she said truthfully, "and confused."

"Michael?"

She nodded. What was that man doing? He blew hotter and colder than a summer night in a snowstorm. She held up the box of pastries for Aaron's inspection and chuckled when Aaron did the same.

"It seems we both have great taste in food, my dear sister. And that man is up to something."

Sarah blushed. "Michael is just a friend; you and I both know that." Would they ever be more?

"I don't know about that. A man doesn't bring breakfast to his brother's sister. He usually brings it to a girl he's interested in."

Was that what Michael was doing? Was that what last night had been about? Unable to form an answer that would satisfy her heart, Sarah curled her hand into Aaron's elbow and allowed him to pull her into the house.

"Whatever the reason, let's get to these before they're cold, shall we?" Aaron's mysterious smile wiggled uneasily in her stomach. Did her brother know something she didn't?

"So, what do you plan on doing today?" Aaron asked.

Biting her lip, Sarah sank down into a nearby barstool. Although the pain medication was doing its magic, her head still felt like a ten-ton weight bearing on her shoulders.

"I need to swing by the community center. Mrs. Rogers said there is a chance that some of the decorations from last year's Christmas pageant could be saved, and we agreed to go and have a look today."

"Didn't the doctor prescribe rest for you?"

"Aaron, the Christmas pageant isn't going to decorate itself; and right now, if anything can be saved, it will be worth investigating."

"I have a busy day at the center, but I could probably make it after lunch and help out."

"That's sweet, but no. Mrs. Rogers said she'll bring her grandson to help with the heavy lifting. We'll be okay."

"If you're sure."

"I'm sure. Thank you for wanting to help."

Aaron nodded. There was new happiness about him. Sarah would bet her last dollar it had something to do with Dakota, Aaron's girlfriend. She was glad to see the two lovebirds had worked things out.

The smell of sawdust and the sound of hammers striking wood met Sarah as she opened the door to the community center. Looking up, she spotted Aaron and Michael high above the ground, working on the eve of the roof. Sarah's stomach trembled with unease at their high perch, only to fizzle into a stampede when Michael's gaze bounced to hers and then back to the hammer. Sarah rolled her eyes. What did she expect? For Michael to fall at her feet and declare his undying love for her? *Only in your dreams, Sarah. Check back in with reality.*

Leaving the men to their work, Sarah shuffled to the decoration room. Her foot ached, and her muscles protested each movement; but as she'd told Aaron, the pageant wouldn't decorate itself. And so, pain aside, she needed to get into those storerooms. She gasped at the mess left behind. Spread over the room were boxes of decoration in various colors and stages of destruction.

"It looks awful, doesn't it?" Mrs. Rogers walked in behind her.

"I didn't realize how bad the damage was."

The older lady frowned. "Most of those decorations have been used for years in the Christmas pageant. I hope some can be salvaged." Sarah nodded.

Wading into the mess, Sarah bent down and opened each box, amazed at the minor damage done to the contents. She glanced over at Mrs. Rogers, who wore an incredulous look Sarah was sure was on her own face. Although the boxes in the far corners were wet and some in the middle looked a tad flat, most of the decorations were intact.

"Oh, oh, oh." Mrs. Rogers clapped her hands softly together and smiled broadly at Sarah. "What a blessing." She opened a few more boxes. "Let me get my grandson; then we can move these out to the church for safekeeping."

Mrs. Rogers came back with a tall, young man who looked no older than seventeen. He smiled shyly at Sarah and followed his grandmother deeper into the room. Sarah checked the contents of a few more. She parted the cardboard shutters. On top lay an angel dressed in blue with dark hair. She smiled serenely at something.

"She looks like you," Michael spoke from behind her.

Sarah startled, the angel wobbling precariously in her hands. "I don't know," she said. "She looks much too peaceful to be me."

There went her brain again. Just being beside him turned her brain to mush. She should be furious after last night's brush-off, but the memory of his kiss made it impossible. No, she couldn't be angry with him.

"How did you sleep?" she asked quietly.

Michael ran his hands through his messy hair. "Better, after . . . " His voice trailed off. His playful expression dissolved as a shadow swept over it.

Sarah sighed. Apparently they were back to that, but she wouldn't accept it. She just needed to remind him of what good friends they'd been before.

"Michael, are we gonna be awkward now?" she asked.

Michael shifted back on his heels. "I don't want to be."

He pressed his lips together and shook his head as if denying something only he could hear.

"Michael?" Sarah reached out for him, stopping when Mrs. Rogers and her grandson walked closer, arms filled with boxes.

"Oh bless, Michael, are you here to help?" Mrs. Rogers exclaimed, oblivious to the tension between them.

"Yes, just for a half-hour or so. Aaron went to get more nails from the shop."

"Well, then, Sarah, dear, you direct him." Mrs. Rogers smiled at her grandson and then winked at Sarah. Perhaps not as oblivious as Sarah thought.

Smiling, she opened another box, overly aware of the man standing beside her. She glanced up and was relieved to see the storm cloud was gone again.

Michael grinned. "Okay, then, direct away."

Sarah chuckled. Insufferable man.

Chapter Eighteen

Michael watched Sarah with admiration as she hobbled from one room to the next, pointing at boxes.

"That one over in the corner," she said. "It should have the tree lights."

In the past half an hour, they'd managed to clean out half the rooms. Sarah and Mrs. Rogers were obviously relieved about the condition of the decorations and the pageant costumes. The pageant was in a few weeks. Thankfully, four of the six rooms had been empty, so the damage in them was minimal. Aaron and his men had pulled the floor up in three of the four and would start on the other three by tomorrow.

Carrying over the last box from room four to the waiting truck outside, Michael smiled at the familiar faces as he passed. Everyone remembered him, and when asked how he was, Michael didn't mind their asking. It was good to be home in Snowy Springs, despite the turmoil caused by a certain brown-eyed lady.

Sarah laughed kindly at something Mrs. Roger's grandson said, and his heart skipped a beat. Their eyes met, and it stole his breath away. She was so beautiful. Why had he never told her how he felt? Aaron. How awkward would it have been for Aaron with Michael dating his sister?

He loved Aaron like a brother. He didn't want to consider what would happen if he hurt her. His mind wandered back to the kiss the night before and quickly skipped over the memory. At the moment, being near her was the only thing that kept him sane. Something that didn't entirely make sense to him. He cleared his throat roughly as the memory of her lips brushed his memory again. Man, he shouldn't have kissed her. But he couldn't bring himself to regret his rash action.

Lucas appeared and gave Sarah a quick hug. Red swept over his vision. With more force than necessary, he slammed the box into the truck. He headed back to Aaron, directing the ground crew to deliver more lumber.

"Are you finished there?" he asked and gestured to his sister.

Michael didn't want to look back, but like a moth drawn to a flame, he turned to follow Aaron's hand. Lucas was nowhere to be seen, and Sarah gestured enthusiastically to something Mrs. Rogers was saying.

"Yeah, I think so. The rooms are empty and are ready for the guys. Did you get those other supplies?"

Aaron nodded. "You wanna help me bring them in?"

Michael turned again. Sarah and Mrs. Rogers had moved off to another room. "Yeah, sure."

The wind howled across the dark gray and brown sky. Heavy snow clouds hung over Snowy Springs waiting to empty their loads and turn Snowy Spring into its namesake. Michael worried another storm would be blowing into town soon. "It's a mess out there," he said.

Aaron looked up briefly and shrugged. "Nothing to worry about— just your average winter's afternoon. Don't worry about it."

But Michael did. It seemed he worried about everything. Lately, small things like time and nail sizes lifted his anxiety levels up to an eleven. A possible snowstorm would push things right off the scale.

"It'll be okay, really," Aaron said as though Michael wore his thoughts open for all to see. "Come on, let's get this stuff unloaded."

Burying his panic, Michael fell in step with Aaron. They dragged the first load of timber from the flatbed. Around them, merry snowflakes fell onto his head and into his eyes. He blinked them away. An indescribable feeling bubbled up from inside him, and a smile caught his lips. Trapped in the moment, he threw his head back, opened his mouth wide, and allowed the snow to fall on his tongue. He found himself chuckling in wonder like a little kid. He'd missed this—the snow, the cold, and the feeling of belonging.

"Man, you have been away too long. Do I leave you here and tell your mom you have wet socks, or are you going to come over here and help me?" Aaron groused.

Michael self-consciously rubbed his neck. "All right, I'm coming."

Movement caught his eye at the entrance to the community center. Sarah stood outside, her arms wrapped around her middle, her gaze locked on him. Joy brimmed from her eyes. Michael grinned, lifted the beam simultaneously with Aaron, and followed him inside. All too aware of her eyes focused on him.

The day had been a long one. Sarah lay stretched out on her mother's soft sofa, grateful to finally be off her feet. Her leg ached along with every place she'd bruised on her trip down the mountain. She groaned softly as the doorbell rang.

"Mom, the door."

"Can you get it, please? This cake will flop if I don't watch it."

"Mom, Aunt Betty's chocolate cake recipe has been used longer than I've been alive. There is no way it'll flop. It never has."

"That's because I've always watched it."

Sighing, she pushed herself to stand and hobbled to the door. Who could be at the door? Aaron and Dakota were working late at the store. And she couldn't think of who else would come over.

In a rush of impatience, someone swung the door open, almost toppling her into the coat closet.

"Lana, are you here?" Michael called.

"No, just Sarah. My mom's watching a cake," she said, peeking her head around the open door.

Michael's eyes widened in surprise before his expression transformed with a heartbreaking smile. "I didn't expect to see you here."

"Same here."

Michael shrugged. "Your mom invited me."

"Oh, she did, did she?" Why did this feel like a setup? *Because no one knows you aren't dating Lucas anymore.* That was true. Maybe it was a happy coincidence.

"How are you feeling today?" Michael asked as he stepped forward to close the door. It was crazy to think how much she'd missed the smell of sandalwood.

"Like I should have listened to my mother and taken today to rest."

The mild amusement turned into laughter.

"Okay, now that you've laughed your pants off at my expense," she said, "what are you really doing here?"

"My, my, ma'am, aren't we forward?" Michael chuckled.

"Did you come here to antagonize me?" That hot bath was sounding better and better by the minute. But first, dinner with her mother.

"I'm serious, Sarah. Lana invited me for dinner," he said.

"That's right. I did," Lana said, walking into the room. "Michael, I'm so glad you could make it."

"What about the cake?" Sarah asked.

"Oh, it's okay." Her mom sounded like a child who had been caught out on a lie. What was her mother up to?

"So, what's for dinner?" Sarah asked, turning and promptly losing her balance. Strong arms slid under hers and held her to a firm chest. Goodness was it hot in here! Her mother nodded knowingly but wisely kept her opinion to herself.

"Lasagna with a Caesar salad."

"No mac and cheese?" Sarah said cheekily, extracting herself from Michael's arms.

"Not tonight," Lana said. "Dinner's almost ready. Why don't you and Michael go sit down until I call you?" Sarah felt her cheeks heat again.

"Do you need some help setting the table?" Michael asked.

Lana shook her head. "It's already done. Now, before Sarah injures herself again, off, you go."

Michael hurried forward to obey her mother's command. A shiver raced up Sarah's spine as he slung his arm low on her hips and gently maneuvered her toward the dining room. The light of the kitchen faded into the background. Sarah was suddenly aware of just how close Michael's body was pressed against hers and, if she was frank with herself, just how nice the feeling was.

"Will you be working tomorrow?" Michael asked. They turned into the dining room. The red tablecloth hung handsomely on the old oak table Sarah had sat around for meals since she was a child. Set for three and with a few candles decorated with Christmas motifs, the meal looked like something out of a Christmas card.

"Yes. Mom's going all out this year," Sarah said. She pointed to the pile of decorations in the corner of the room.

"It's not every Christmas one of your sons returns," her mother said from behind them. Michael lifted his arm from around Sarah to help bring in the dishes her mother carried. She felt the loss acutely. When the table was ladened with her mother's delicious lasagna, salad, and warm garlic bread, they sat.

"Michael, would you say the grace?" Lana requested and took Sarah's hand. Her mom had encouraged Michael to sit at the table's head and seated Sarah on the left and herself on the right. Sarah wasn't sure how she felt about it but let it slide. As long as her mother was happy.

Michael held out his hand; another tingle shivered through her as she laid her hand in his. After grasping her mother's hand, Michael blessed the food in a low, quiet voice that Sarah could listen to for hours. Oh dear, there she went again.

Once dinner was over, and Michael left, Sarah slowly drove home, thankful for automatic cars. Michael starred in her every thought as the events of the evening played around in her memory. She remembered the times they'd spent together growing up and sighed at the people they'd been then. Her shy and awkward eagerness to be anywhere Michael was and him oblivious with one date after another. And yet, Michael had always had a way of making her feel welcome, memorable, and wanted. That was the reason, she guessed, her enormous crush on him had developed.

Leave it alone, Sarah; it's the past. Silly as it sounded, it didn't feel that way.

Chapter Nineteen

"So, this is what you've been getting up to." Michael halted his hammer and looked down. His thoughts were on the night before, his hand mechanically completing his task. Noah was below him, head titled back, concern lining his face. Michael carefully grasped the long ladder suspended at the bottom eve and descended it.

"Not that I'm not glad to see you, but what are you doing here?" Michael asked, taking his brother into a swift hug.

"You don't call; you don't write. We were beginning to worry about you."

Michael shrugged. "I'm doing all right." Since that night where he'd kissed Sarah, something in his dust-dry heart had come to life again. Something that gave him hope. Although Sarah was with Lucas, there was a connection between them. It was unexplainable, the magnetism between them. He was sure Sarah felt it, too.

The knocking in the room continued around them. Michael had become so accustomed to his colleagues' enthusiasm with hammers that it only bugged him every now and then. He lifted the next board onto his shoulder and leaned it against the foot of the ladder, ready to hoist it up.

The door to the community center opened. A fissure of pleasure shot through him as Sarah walked into the room. His expression must have shown his delight because Noah turned and followed his gaze.

"Ah, I see the reason for your better mood. Sarah?"

The incredulity in his brother's voice made Michael want to smack him. What did he know, anyway?

As if she could sense their discussion, Sarah turned and caught his eye, a shy smile on those soft lips. For a moment, he forgot who held company with him and got lost in the moment. A rough clearing of a throat brought him back to reality and right into Noah's smirking face. Caught red-handed.

"Knock it off; she has a boyfriend." He grabbed his hammer and lumbered off to the supply station to take another pack of nails, effectively ignoring his chuckling brother. Many hours of hard work had gone into the community center roof, but there was still much work to do. The other rooms' damage had been more extensive than Aaron had initially thought, and the constant waves of snow weren't doing anything to help the situation.

"Ah-ha." Noah smiled guilelessly at him and walked around the construction site. "If you say so."

"Did you come with a purpose or just to be a pain in the butt?"

"I told you, I came to check on you."

"You could've used a phone for that."

Noah sighed. "I tried. You didn't answer."

Guilt ate at him. But for the hurried call with his parents, he hadn't answered any calls or emails from his family. It was easier that way, although he regretted it every now and then.

"Okay, Mom wants you to come back to Denver," Noah said.

"I'll visit." Silence.

Noah watched him with an ambivalent expression. "She wants you back in Denver for good."

"I can't. Noah, I can't explain the noise, the people. The expectations . . ."

"What do you mean you can't? What aren't you telling us, Michael? You're back after three years. You were in Denver barely long enough to say a proper hello, and then you were gone again. Do you know how Mom and Dad felt when we got the call? We thought you were dead, Michael. It almost ripped the family apart. Mom and Dad were the worst I have ever seen them. It took months for them to recover."

Michael took a deep, pained breath and closed his eyes. "I'm sorry, Noah. I just can't. I promise I'll make a plan to visit soon. I need more time."

"Time to do what?"

"I don't know. All I know is that I can't go back there." How could he explain to Noah? The gut-wrenching fear that seized him each day and left him awake for hours each night in Denver seemed to be getting easier in Snowy Springs. The idea of leaving the familiarity of Snowy Springs and Sarah nearly brought him to his knees. Anxiety chewed at him, and the only person who seemed to bring it to heel was standing on the other side of the room talking to Aaron.

Noah nodded sympathetically. "Okay, Bro, I'll explain that to them, but you should call them and tell them yourself."

"I will when I'm ready." A silent promise he made himself, he would phone his parents when he could.

"You guys have your work cut out for you here?" Noah asked and looked around the room. His eyes followed the path of the roof.

Michael, relieved the guilt trip was over, slung his hammer into his belt and picked up the board. "Yeah, too much work and too little time." He glanced at Sarah, who was now surrounded by a group of ladies. Each one's head was bent close, mesmerized by her. Perhaps it was only he who thought so. Sarah could be wearing a potato sack, and the effect would be the same.

"Come on, Romeo, that board isn't going to set itself," Noah teased. Ignoring his brother's knowing look, Michael shimmied up the ladder and over to the most damaged part of the roof. Ironically, the ceiling and he had a lot in common, both damaged and in desperate need of repair. Except the fixing he needed was a lot deeper and more extensive than a few broken struts and board. And his construction crew were out to lunch.

The board lined up flawlessly against the rafter. He positioned one nail at a time and hammered them in with precise movements. He lost himself in the rhythm. Thoughts of family and their unmet expectations dragged like heavy weight on his limbs. He'd missed them and hated to leave them again, but the constant waves of concern strangled him. And the thought of them seeing how mangled he was from his time overseas . . . He sighed. There was only so long that he could keep up the façade, no matter how much his parents loved him.

Noah stayed around and chatted to the town's folk catching up. Michael saw him do a double-step and freeze as a small, dark-haired woman came into the room. Michael couldn't see her features; but whoever it was, Noah's friendly expression altered into a deep scowl, and he marched out of the community center at an alarming pace. What on earth?

The remainder of the afternoon passed with a dizzying speed, and sometime in the last few minutes, knocking-off time had happened. Michael collected his things and packed away the tools so that everything would be ready for the next day. Order helped. It lessened the anxiety he felt each morning when coming to work.

Noah stormed over to him, his face a rigid mask. He circled Michael a few times before sighing loudly and leaning against the nearest wall.

"Something on your mind?" Michael asked.

Noah shook his head vigorously. "Nothing I want to talk about."

"Are you sure? Because you look like you need to."

"How could she . . . When did she . . . " His lips clapped together in a firm line, a deep sorrow lining his brow. "Never mind," he whispered hoarsely.

Michael watched his brother. "If you're sure . . . " Another nod. "So, I hear Ben has a rodeo nearby tomorrow. Do you wanna go?"

"Yeah, the circuit has been kind to him in the last few weeks."

"Do you think Drew can make it?"

A shadow of a smile lifted Noah's cheek. "Anywhere there's food, Drew will be. I never could understand why he can go to the hottest restaurants in town and still like the fried food at the rodeo. It boggles the mind."

Michael chuckled. "Let's head on out. Are you here for the night, or are you driving back?"

"Why? Do you have plans?"

Michael would love to have had plans with a certain young lady, but seeing as she probably already had plans with Lucas, Noah would have to do. "Nope, just me and pizza to keep me company tonight."

"You sure?"

"Yep."

Noah glanced around the room. Michael knew Sarah had left ages ago. He noticed everything about her, including how often she'd looked his way that afternoon. He suppressed the wave of jealously. The memory of those soft lips compelled the emotion in him. *Stop it, Michael; she's taken.* If only he could. Sarah was with him when he woke up in the middle of the night, sweat from nightmares drenching his body. That was when he'd remember her soft scent, those pouty lips, and her warm, brown eyes laughing into his. The demon would turn tail and run in the wake of the peace she brought him.

"Okay, pizza it is. Papa Paulo?"

"Still the best." Michael laughed and followed Noah out into the dark afternoon.

They arrived back at Michael's apartment at almost the same time. Michael climbed out of his truck, surprised to see the lights of the bookstore burning.

"Hang on a minute. I want to check on Lana."

With Sarah injured, Lana had been doing the lion's share of work at the bookstore for the past few days while Sarah did her best to control the community center's Christmas plans.

The two men entered the bookstore. There was no one at the counter, but a light shone from the back storeroom.

"Lana," Michael muttered, tilting his head toward the back of the store. Noah nodded and walked almost silently behind him. There was a heavy thump followed by a cry of pain. Michael rushed forward in full alert. Sarah sat on a nearby chair in the storeroom and rubbed her injured leg. A box of books lay on its side at her feet.

"What are you doing here?" he asked, coming to her aid. Sarah's head lifted in alarm, quickly replaced by relief. "Are you okay?"

"You know I work here, right?" she said dryly. Noah barked a laugh as Michael bent down beside her.

"Funny. I thought you were taking some time off," Michael said. He wrapped his hand lightly around her injured limb and rubbed gently.

"I wanted to, but you know Mom." A sweet color filled Sarah's cheeks as she gazed down at him. A man could get lost in those deep brown eyes.

Suddenly, Sarah inhaled sharply and broke the tie. He was in severe trouble. *Remember she has a boyfriend, Michael.* Roughly clearing his throat, he helped Sarah to her feet and bent to help her with the box.

"How can we help?"

Sarah glanced over his shoulder, the color in her cheeks burning brighter. Michael cursed. He'd forgotten Noah was behind him, and he could only imagine what was going through his brother's mind.

"These boxes need to go to the storefront. I almost had it when my leg gave way, and I dropped the box."

"Okay, Noah and I can do that. Why don't you give me the key and go on home? I'll lock up and give it to whomever comes to the store first, or I can drop it off."

"It'll be me. Mom won't be in for the next few days. Her arthritis has flared up again."

"Is there anything else we can do?" he asked.

"Helping with boxes will be more than enough. It's just those five." Sarah motioned to an array of boxes laid beside the door of the storeroom.

In short order, he and Noah moved the boxes to the storefront under Sarah's watchful eyes.

"Sarah, we're about to get pizza. Want to come?" Noah asked.

Michael stiffened. The little . . . Michael would happily break both his legs. Noah wouldn't be such a pain if he couldn't walk. Noah smiled mischievously, pressing his luck.

Sarah smiled graciously and said, "Not tonight but thanks for the offer. Mom is waiting for me."

After a quick goodbye to Sarah, Michael dragged Noah in a headlock up to his apartment. He wasn't angry, just embarrassed by the sheer guile of his brother.

Noah thrust Michael forward, disengaging the headlock and laughing. "She has a boyfriend, indeed. Any other lies you wanna tell me?"

Noah was definitely finding dirt in his sheets tonight.

Chapter Twenty

"I'm glad you could make it tonight," Ben said and fixed his arm securely around his wife's waist. Susie was as round with child as a grape and just as sweet. How Juliet and Susie came from the same family still befuddled him. They were as opposite as day and night. Anyway, he was happy for his brother.

"Well, you've been hammerin' on us for the last few weeks that you'd be in town. I figured the least we could do was make an effort to come," Michael replied.

Drew sniffed loudly; rodeo was not his idea of fun. He'd come only for the food. Noah talked to someone in the background and then walked back over to them. "Hey, Michael, did you know Aaron would be here tonight?"

"Yeah, he mentioned he and Sarah would be coming with that new boyfriend of hers."

"New boyfriend?" Noah raised an eyebrow.

"Don't start, dude," Michael warned.

Noah grinned. "I've got nothing to say."

"Good, let's keep it that way."

"Are you two done?" Drew asked. "Hey, Ben, is the food here any good?"

"Well, as good as you can get at any rodeo. I've gotta get ready. I'll see you after." He quickly said his goodbyes, and he and Susie disappeared into the bull-riders' section.

Michael scanned the arena. It looked just the same as he remembered. Hundreds, if not thousands, of people stood or sat in the stands talking, laughing, or eating. All around him were cowboy hats, checkered shirts, and cowboy boots. The fluorescent lights reminded him of the enormous spotlights they'd used back at the base and in the desert. No, not tonight.

So many things he'd never suspected would trigger the memories. Loud noises and the smell of fire, dust, and gun powder brought all his worst memories back in a rush.

Take it easy, Michael. Deep breaths.

And breathe he did—long and deep.

"You okay?" Noah asked.

"Yeah, yeah, fine."

Noah nodded. He was concerned.

Michael was beginning to hate that look. He saw it all too often in his brothers' faces. They worried about him. He worried about himself. When the nightmares didn't come at night, they'd come during the day. When he was busy on the roof, they'd strike. All he could do was hold on tight to something and go along for the ride. It seemed no amount of calling, yelling, or shaking could bring him back to reality. The last one had been horrible. He'd been busy at the apex of the roof, lining up frames, when one of the other guys had used the nail gun. Instantly, Michael had found himself back in his cell, sweat dripping down his body and pain knifing his arms and legs. Thank goodness, Aaron had been there to catch him, or it would've been his end.

He scrubbed his hand through his hair and replaced his cowboy hat, stamping his boots. *Concentrate on something else, Michael.* If he was going to make it through tonight, he had to soldier up.

"You want something to eat before we find our seats?" Noah asked, ready to follow Drew into the food tent.

Eat? His stomach was clenched in a hard knot. He doubted food would do anything to soothe it. "Nah, just something to drink."

Together, the brothers strolled toward the tent when light laughter caught Michael's attention.

"Hey, Mike," Aaron said.

"Hey, you guys just get here?"

"Yeah. Missy over here had a clothing issue." Aaron gestured to Sarah.

Sarah blushed bright red. It was beautiful to see. "Whatever. I couldn't find my boots. I can't remember the last time I wore these." She showed off the leather boots that started below her knees. Sarah had great legs, and in those blue jeans . . .

Michael shifted his attention back to her face. Brown hair fell in curly waves down her shoulders, and man, tonight, she chose to wear red. A color he'd always thought looked great on her. "So, where's the other guy?" he asked.

Aaron glanced over at Sarah, who looked back and then at Michael. "Ah, he's not coming."

"I'm surprised he let you out of his sight that long," Michael muttered. Lucas was probably a good guy, and the only reason Michael didn't like him was Sarah. Well, he wasn't going to look a gift horse in the mouth. Tonight, Sarah was on her own, and he would enjoy spending time in her company for the only reason he could honestly tell himself—because he wanted to.

After stopping to grab some food and a few water bottles, the group made their way up the bleachers. Michael tightly gripped his water bottle until the plastic groaned in protest. The showtime noise was crushing. Below, the women had begun barrel racing. Ben's wife, Susie, had been an avid barrel racer until an injury had forced her to stop. It was also the place Ben and Susie had met.

"Can you still ride?" he asked Sarah as she walked up the stairs silently beside him.

"Me? No. Once was enough. It wasn't something I wanted to repeat."

Michael couldn't help but smile. He knew exactly what Sarah was referring to. When Michael and Aaron were seventeen, they'd decided they wanted to be cowboys for the summer. They'd signed up to work at a nearby ranch helping out with horses and crops. After learning to ride and a misguided attempt to get Sarah out of her books, they'd tried to take her horseback riding with disastrous results. Their plan hadn't worked, and Sarah had fallen off the back of the placid, old nag they had put her on. Sarah walked away with bruises and a healthy respect for horses. She'd been so mad at them, it had taken weeks to get back into her good graces.

Sarah grinned. Michael couldn't help reaching out and touching her hand as they shared the memory. All too soon, they'd come to their seats, and the closeness of the moment was over. Michael sat between Noah and Drew while Aaron protectively placed his sister on his other side, away from Michael. Best friend or not, Aaron was a big brother through and through.

"Hey, Michael, didn't you say you wanted to check out those horses on the south side of the tent?" Noah asked, scarfing a large bag of peanuts.

"Yeah, I will after Ben is done riding."

Noah nodded and then tipped his head in Sarah's direction.

"There's a beautiful thoroughbred mare I'm sure Sarah would love to see."

What are you doing, Noah?

Noah smiled at him, his eyes dancing with mischief. Great, so Noah wanted to play matchmaker.

"I'm sure if Sarah wanted to see the horse, she'd ask Aaron to take her," he said, a warning clear in the tone of his voice. Aaron raised his eyebrow. Michael shook his head before looking over to Sarah again. She was entranced by the barrel racers below and hadn't noticed the contest of wills going. Aaron slit his eye at Michael in a warning and then nodded.

"Sarah, do you want to go see that mare we talked about?" Aaron asked his sister.

"What? Oh, yeah. I'd love to see her."

Michael stood. Sarah's face momentarily clouded with confusion before she, too, stood. "Are you coming with me?" she asked him.

"If that's okay?" he asked.

"Ah, sure. Aaron?"

"I'll catch up with you." He glanced at Michael again, his message clear. *Look after her.*

Sarah stepped out of the row, followed by Michael. Together, they walked toward the stalls at the back of the arena. Michael followed Sarah out from the competition area and into the large group of stables in the back. Sarah walked, seemingly lost in thought.

"Penny for 'em?" he said as they came to the entrance.

"Huh?"

"Your thoughts? Where are you?"

Sarah sighed. "Oh, I was just thinking about that time you and Aaron tried to teach me to ride."

"I was just thinking about the same thing. Do you remember how you tipped off that nag?"

Sarah laughed. "You wouldn't believe why I fell off. It wasn't because I misstepped." She blushed. "Anyway, it was funny."

All around them, various types of thoroughbreds, geldings, and mustangs waited in every color imaginable. A tall palomino stamped his hoof, defiantly staring at the door. "So, what was the reason?" he asked.

"Never mind, I don't think it's important anymore." There was something she wasn't telling him.

"What was it, Sarah?" he asked, stopping her with a hand to her arm. Sarah paused, her deep brown eyes turned up to his, filled with some emotion he couldn't decipher.

"Am I interrupting something?" Aaron had arrived.

"Impeccable timing as usual," Sarah muttered. But to Michael, his friend's timing just stunk.

"See anything interesting in there?"

Was he wrong to be mad at his friend? Michael slipped his hands into his back pockets and pretended to concentrate on the tack that hung over one for the stable doors.

"Where's Dakota?" Sarah asked.

"She wasn't feeling well; I think she caught the flu. She's helping Mrs. Delmonte out with her granddaughter, and the little one was sick a few days ago."

"That's a shame; I was looking forward to seeing her."

Loud cheering came from the main arena as they announced the winners of the first round of barrel riding. "And now, ladies and gentleman, please help me welcome the Western Cowboys. They're here to entertain us before we begin our next event, the bull-riding," the announcer said over the intercom. A wave of noise drowned out whatever he said next.

"I guess we'd better get back," Aaron said, guiding Sarah to the entrance of the stables. Michael followed miserably.

The lights were low as they entered the arena. Without warning, a giant spotlight broke the darkness, followed by a series of loud bangs. The smell of gun powder and dirt seared Michael's nose. His heart rate quickened as his memories dragged him back to another time, deep in a cold, dank, concrete hole.

Loud shouting in Pashto filled his ears and drove the memory deeper. The heat of the forsaken desert scorched his pale flesh. No, this time, they wouldn't take him. Immersed in his memory, Michael swung his fists and collided with bodies in front of him. He kept on with all his might, even as hands reached out to him, followed by more and more shouting. Strong arms grabbed him and tried to drag him down. He wouldn't go back into the hole, not while he had breath left in his body. He fought back. Another pair of strong arms grabbed around his middle.

"Michael," someone shouted, but he didn't know the voice. No one spoke English where he was. More lights flashed as he fought, the arms around him more frantic in their pursuit.

"Michael . . ."

Chapter Twenty-One

The horror of the past few minutes slowly faded as Michael came out of the nightmare.

"Michael."

"Michael."

"Michael, can you hear me?" Sarah asked. Her desperation bled into her words. With unsteady legs, she stepped closer. "Michael, come back to us."

The agonized muttering continued until Michael froze. The painful set of his shoulders relaxed, and his rigid body went limp between his brothers. Drew and Noah eased the death grip on Michael's arms while Aaron released the bear hold he had on Michael's torso.

"It's okay, man. You're okay now," he said tiredly.

Michael's ragged breath punctuated the tense silence. Noah, Drew, and Aaron had managed to guide a struggling Michael into a relatively unpopulated area of the arena during the scuffle. Nobody outside of the stables was aware of the tempest thrashing inside. She leaned forward and cupped Michael's rough cheeks between her hands. "Michael. Look at me. Can you hear me?"

Sarah couldn't fathom why Noah thought her voice would be the one to reach Michael when the others couldn't. But for whatever reason, it had worked. Michael's anguished groans subsided, and his loud, labored breathing returned to normal. Weakly, he pushed

Aaron and Noah back and covered Sarah's hands with his own. His eyes remained closed as his warmth sank into her.

"Michael, you're safe. It's okay; you are safe. Can you hear me?"

"Yes," he rasped. "Yes, Sarah, I can hear you."

Sweet relief flowed into her. His trembling hands squeezed hers one last time and fell away, "Yes, I can hear you." Michael's legs gave way beneath him, and he collapsed in a heap at her feet, unconscious.

Noah, Drew, and Aaron jumped into action. They looped their arms under Michael's and dragged him back to his feet. He didn't fight. It looked like he didn't have any fight left in him. Sarah took a deep breath. She was cold, as cold as her empty hands. The truth she'd known for so long rang out in her heart. With a reluctant sigh, she acknowledged it. She was still in love with Michael. Aaron and Noah dragged Michael between them as Sarah stood and caught her breath.

"Sarah, are you coming?" Aaron called from the door of the stables.

She nodded and hurried after her brother, catching up with them quickly. In a quiet procession, they hauled Michael into the silent night and to Noah's waiting truck. Michael was so pale, and yet his features were relaxed, almost peaceful. She hoped he was.

"Let me take him," Noah said. "Levi's at Grandma's house. He says it's probably a good idea that when he comes to, it's somewhere familiar."

Leave him? Everything in her wanted to protest, although Levi probably knew what he was talking about.

Aaron nodded, and she did the same. "Please let us know how he is."

Walking around the other men, she opened the door by Michael's head. His breathing was shallow and slow. She ran her hand over the sweat droplets on his forehead.

"Oh, Michael," she whispered and placed a quick kiss on his cheek. "Please be okay."

She walked back to her brother just in time to hear Noah say, "We will and thanks." Drew came forward and shook Aaron's hand; he gave Sarah a quick hug. "He'll be okay," he reassured them. "He's in good hands."

Oh, Lord, please let him be okay, Sarah prayed. The ache, like physical pain, burrowed deep in her heart. Michael had been in so much pain. She wished she knew how to soothe it. With a salute, the two brothers climbed into the truck and drove off.

Aaron sighed and scrubbed the back of his neck. "I'll call Ben from the road," he said and ran back into the arena. Sarah waited outside in the pitch dark and listened to the cheering sounds that came from inside. The fun side of the evening seemed a lifetime ago. A few minutes later, Aaron returned with their coats and some of the other men's stuff ladened over his arms.

"I hope I have everything," he said.

"I'm sure we can call tomorrow if we don't." She was exhausted. Her emotions were spent from the struggle with Michael. Another prayer whispered from her heart. Michael had to be okay. The crowd roared in the arena again, and Sarah was startled. Was this how Michael felt? Like he stood on the outside looking in? If it was, it was a scary place to be. She swung her coat over her shoulders, thankful for the warmth it provided her cold body, and wrapped herself deeper into it. Aaron opened his truck door for her, and she climbed in. The opposite door creaked open and closed as he climbed in beside her. There was silence in the cab, broken only by the mournful music on the radio.

Aaron turned on the truck. "You okay?"

"I think so. I didn't expect it. What happened to him? One moment we were together talking, and then I don't know what happened . . . "

Aaron reached over the squeezed her shoulder. "He'll be fine. Michael is made of strong stuff."

"I hope so. Oh, Aaron, what if . . . " She cut herself off. *What if* wasn't going to help anyone. Aaron put the truck in drive and turned onto the main road leading back to Snowy Springs. Sarah curled into a ball and processed the images racing through her mind in a scary parade. *Help him, Lord.*

"Are you still in love with him?"

Would it help to deny it? She couldn't, not any longer.

"Sarah, I know about your high school crush on Michael. I never said anything because, well, he's my best friend and you're my sister. But the look on your face . . . "

It was no use. Not anymore. "Yes."

Aaron glanced at her quizzically. "Really?"

"Aaron . . . "

Aaron grinned and toggled the switch on the radio. "The heart wants what the heart wants."

Yes, it did. Sarah sighed and closed her eyes. Her mind was always on Michael. What had happened tonight? Where had he gone?

"We're a fine pair, aren't we?"

Aaron laughed. "Yeah. You about ready to go home?"

"Yeah, although I don't think I'll sleep until Drew phones. I did get a new book, so . . . " Laughter filled the cabin and released some of the earlier tension.

"You and your books," Aaron teased.

"Better than any movie. You should try it sometime."

"Whatever." Aaron smiled and tapped her forehead. "I'll leave the smart stuff to you."

They stopped outside Sarah's bungalow, and Sarah climbed out. "Let me know if you hear anything, okay?" she asked as she closed the door.

"Will do." Aaron waved and drove off.

After a long, hot bath and too much ice cream, Sarah made ready for bed. Despite her bone-deep exhaustion, she couldn't seem to get her mind to shut down long enough to relax. Her new book was already halfway done, and if she kept on reading, it was likely she wouldn't get any sleep. Why wasn't Drew calling her? Was Michael still passed out? Had something else happened?

Stop borrowing trouble, Sarah.

Drew would phone her when he had something to tell her. She knew him well enough to know that. Maybe she should just recheck her phone. Nothing. It was time to bring out the big guns—warm milk with honey. Shuffling down to the kitchen, Sarah quickly warmed the milk, added some honey, and reclimbed the stairs to her bedroom. She slowly sipped the warm concoction and paged through the pages of her Bible. Maybe the verses would calm the anxiety in her heart.

Flipping to Psalm 34:1-10, she read, *"I will extol the Lord at all times; his praise will always be on my lips . . . I sought the Lord, and he answered me; he delivered me from all my fears. Those who look to him are radiant . . . The angel of the Lord encamps around those who fear him, and he delivers them . . . Taste and see that the Lord is good; blessed is the one who takes refuge in him . . . those who seek the Lord lack no good thing."*

Closing the Bible to wipe the droplets on her cheeks, Sarah sighed. God would be with Michael. She just had to trust Him.

Chapter Twenty-Two

Michael awoke with a start, instantly aware. Where was he? And where was Sarah? Was she hurt? A tumble of memories vied for attention around the clear image of her face. Soft, brown eyes and her sweet voice called to him in the madness. Michael rubbed his scruffy face and pushed himself off the bed. His alarm slowly faded as his eyes fell on the old quilt he knew was in his grandma's guest room. Why was he at Grandma's? And more importantly, how did he get there? His memory shifted to the familiar faces of his brothers. Noah, Ben, and Drew had been with him. Where were they now?

As he walked across the hall to the bathroom, soft voices rose from the level below. They were all downstairs. He glanced back at the trail of dust following him. He was filthy. How did that happen?

Grit and sand crunched under his feet as he entered the bathroom and turned on the light. He definitely needed to shower. The water came on with a powerful hiss and quickly steamed up the room. Michael shucked his dirty clothes and climbed in. He groaned as the blistering spray poured down his body. Something stung his back where his scars were. He must've knocked against something and opened the wounds again. Brown and red-tinted water flowed down the shower drain. What had happened to him?

His body felt like he'd gone four rounds with a bucking horse. A dull ache became apparent in his shoulders, and he was surprised to see a collection of minor purple marks on his upper arms, along with a band around his chest. Aaron joined the montage of Drew and Noah tackling him to the ground. He'd watched them do it and yet was powerless to stop the blind rage. Sighing, he turned off the rapidly cooling water and dried off.

Now fully clothed, Michael sank down onto the edge of the bed. His secret was out for all to see. How would he face Sarah? How would his brothers react after last night? They'd probably want to lock him in an asylum after witnessing the extent of his madness.

The door opened with a single tap, and Noah entered the room.

"Michael?"

"Not now," he muttered.

"Michael, are you awake? We heard the shower."

Lifting his face from his cupped hands, Michael glanced over at this brother. "I'm awake." He wished Noah would just leave him alone, hoped everyone would.

"Please just leave me alone," he said.

Noah limped closer and sat beside him. "You need help, Bro. No amount of denial or hope is going to make the dreams and suffering go away. Believe me, I know."

Michael sat back down on the bed, his head in his hands, blood pounding through his veins. "I know," he whispered.

Noah shifted and straightened his injured leg in front of him. "You are my brother, and I love you. Don't keep doing this to yourself. Soldiering up each time you're about ready to wet your pants from fear. That's not a life. You can't keep running." He sighed softly. "Please, man. If you can't do it for yourself, think about Sarah." Noah clapped him on the shoulder as he stood. "We're waiting for you downstairs when you're ready."

Michael sat staring at the wall for a long while. Noah was right, and Levi had been right from the start. If he didn't find some way to deal with his pain, he wouldn't live any kind of life. He'd be stuck in the darkness forever. And Sarah? He couldn't think about Sarah. If she needed any more convincing that Lucas was the right one for her, she had it.

The stairs creaked under his feet as he walked down them. Six sets of eyes turned toward the sound. Michael paused in the threshold. Sarah, Aaron, Drew, Noah, Levi, and his grandma watched him with expressions ranging from apprehension to relief, and well, he wasn't sure what lingered in Sarah's eyes. Memories of the night before slammed into him. Shame and guilt twisted his gut as he walked into the room.

He couldn't find a smile today, not even a pretend one. Everyone was probably waiting for him to go psycho again. Sarah rose to her feet from the sofa, her luminant eyes filled with compassion, and walked over to him. Michael stepped back; a wave of irrational anger stormed into his calm. What right did she have to look at him like that? Didn't she have a boyfriend? Shouldn't that kind of mercy be saved for someone she loved?

"What are you doing here?" he asked viciously. He pulled himself up to his full height and thrust his shoulders back. Angry and untouchable. It lasted for a heartbeat.

Sarah stopped, her face filled with compassion. "We came to see how you were doing," she said softly. Aaron stood warily behind her, his expression filled with the same understanding.

Red clouded Michael's eyes. What was left of his rational mind screamed for him to stop, but it was no use. "Yeah, well, as you can see, I'm fine. I'm fine. Can't everyone see? I'm fine. I just want to be left alone without someone looking at me like I'm some kind of injured animal."

"Michael." Sarah stood bold and proud in the face of his rage. The awareness crushed his anger, and shame quickly took its place. What was he doing? Michael closed his eyes and sank back down into the sofa.

"Michael," Sarah said again. The cushion beside him gave way under her as she sat. He felt her small hand circle his and reluctantly opened his eyes. The room was empty.

"They're waiting outside to give us some privacy," Sarah said.

Privacy? What did they need privacy for? Realization hit him. She was going to tell him to leave her alone. That she didn't want to see him again. He tugged his hand away, but Sarah held firm.

"Michael," Sarah said yet again.

Cool hands firmly cupped his hot cheeks and forced his eyes down to hers. His emotions turned into a snarled knot as she gazed at him. Sarah sighed and then pushed closer. The soft, soothing touch of her lips that should have brought calm had the opposite effect. His desperation boiled over. He thrust her away from him and walked to the far side to get away from her.

"No, Sarah. Go back to Lucas." The words cut him like a blazing knife, pain thrust into his heart.

"Lucas isn't the one I want, Michael—the man I want to love," she said sadly and moved in his direction again. Michael shied away from her, almost cringing out of her reach. Sarah's footsteps faltered, agony in her eyes.

"I can't love you, Sarah; I'm broken. I'll never be able to love anyone. Go back to Lucas. You don't want a man like me."

His words must've finally hit home because the brown eyes he loved so much filled with tears. "If that's what you want, Michael," she said.

"It is," he said. His feet led him out the room, past his brothers' sympathetic faces, past Aaron, and past his grandma out into the cold winter's afternoon.

He gasped as another wave of pain struck his heart. Sarah. Now, more than ever, he wished he could turn back time and be the man Sarah remembered. Levi and Noah's words echoed right into his heart. He needed help. He could never be any good to anyone if he didn't get it.

One by one, they followed him out. Noah whistled under his breath as he took the crate opposite him. "Aaron is madder than a nest of hornets. What did you do to Sarah?"

"Something I should have done a long time ago," he said mournfully. He should have stayed away from Sarah. He never should have let things get so far with them under the guise of friendship. It had only hurt her. He blew out a deep breath. "I need to leave Snowy Springs. All I'm doing here is hurting people. Maybe one day, she'll forgive me."

Drew and Noah nodded, their relief evident. Until that moment, he hadn't known the strain he'd put his family under with his unwillingness to deal with his PTSD.

"Your old room is available at Mom and Dad's," Levi said. "I could use a handyman around the church—if you're interested, that is."

Michael cracked a smile. "Thanks, I'd appreciate it. Wait, what about the community center?"

Noah grinned. "I'll tell Aaron. Once we've explained, he'll understand. I've got to do something to keep you safe from yourself."

He hated leaving Aaron in the lurch. Aaron might understand about the community center, but he doubted he would about Sarah. Another pang struck his heart. It was for the best. Sarah deserved better than half a man. Lost in thought, he didn't notice Grandma walking out into the yard, her hands ladened with a tray. They all stood to their feet, Drew taking the tray.

Grandma smiled at each of them. "Now, not that I don't enjoy having you boys here, but what is the fuss all about? And, Michael, why is that girl crying? Did you do something to her?"

He felt his cheeks warm. "Yes, Grandma. She doesn't need me. She deserves someone better than a raving lunatic."

Grandma clicked her tongue sternly, although he could see the twinkle in her eye. "Michael, you mustn't say those things. That girl would be blessed to have a man like you. Now, stop your fussin' and make an old lady some tea."

Michael glanced around. Noah hid a grin behind his hand; Drew and Levi smiled openly. "Yes, Grandma."

"And once you've done that, you can go and clean that mess you left in the bathroom. Boy, how did your mama raise you? She'd be shocked to see the mess."

"Yes, Grandma," he said with a groan. His brothers were positively paralytic with laughter. Michael smiled, and then chuckled, and then began to laugh along. Nobody said no to Grandma.

Chapter Twenty-Three

Misery loved company, or so they said. Sarah wasn't so sure. She sat perched on the balcony at the ski lodge and watched the waves of colors ebb and flow down the slopes. Juliet and Callen had somehow coerced her into coming today. She wasn't sure why she'd said yes. Skiing was the last thing she wanted to do. It reminded her too much of Michael. And yet, Juliet had dragged her out here with the promise that exercise was therapeutic. Sarah knew the value of activity, but she didn't see the need for it in her current situation.

Michael had left town. And what was Sarah doing? Working herself to a standstill in an attempt to hide her misery. Laboring at the bookstore for hours seemed like a delightful idea compared to ice in her snowpants. She spent every waking hour either at the store or at the community center, roughing it with the guys in a rush to get everything done before Christmas Eve. Aaron had made a few comments about her hours, same as her mother. She'd grimaced and told them to mind their own business.

This morning, when Juliet had turned up at her house, she had demanded Sarah come out with them. If Sarah didn't love her friend so much and understand why she thought she was helping, Sarah might have told her the same thing. Her phone rang. She glanced at the caller ID. Aaron again. Her brother was becoming a worrywart.

Maybe she'd talk to Dakota. Sarah was sure Dakota could find better uses for her brother's time than worrying about his sister.

"Yes, Aaron," she said, exasperation coloring her tone.

"Hey, Sarah, where are you? You said you were meeting us at eleven."

"Oh, so she didn't tell you. Juliet kidnapped me this morning. I'm at Echo Ridge, enjoying the luscious cold."

"Now, I know you aren't serious. Where are you?"

"In Echo Ridge, sipping hot chocolate and staring at the snow."

"Really?"

"Really, really. So, if that's all . . . " Sarah swiped her phone and ended the call. Aaron was like a mother hen. Avery—bless her heart—was too busy to worry about Sarah, and Sarah was grateful. She loved her family, but since the Michael fiasco, Aaron had become slightly overbearing, and she knew Avery didn't care for Michael, so maybe it was best she wasn't involved.

She sighed as she sat back into her chair and picked up the book resting on her lap. Books used to always be a wonderful escape for her. Now, each time she picked up one, the hero invariably resembled Michael in some way. Just like her current one was turning out to be.

Frustrated, she closed the book and looked out onto the snow. It was useless. There was no getting away from him or the pain in her heart. She found herself in the same position as she had in the days that followed Michael's deployment, only this time he had kissed her. Sarah twisted her fingers together. That one kiss had created a new avalanche of pain that she hadn't seen coming. She should've.

"Hey, Sarah." Sarah stood up; Juliet was under the balcony, her wild, red hair tamed by the large band around her head.

"Yes?"

"Are you going to sit up there the whole day?"

"I'm considering it."

"So, do I need to resort to some kind of scare tactic to get you down here?"

Sarah thought for a moment. "No, I'll be down in a minute." Moping wasn't getting her anywhere. Maybe it was time to take another shot at dealing with her pain in a more productive way.

Sarah packed her things and placed her backpack in the locker. She put on her snow gear and hurried out to where Juliet waited with skis and poles in hand. Her injured ankle twinged as she fastened the clips on her boots, and she wiggled it around to set the foot more comfortably.

Juliet smiled as she approached. "That's my girl."

"I should've seen this coming, Jules," Sarah said as she snapped in her skis.

Juliet patted her shoulder. "How could you stop it?" She sighed and pulled Sarah over to another set of chairs. "Why didn't you tell me? Sarah, you've been my best friend since kindergarten. I thought you were over your Michael episode. When Lucas came, I couldn't have been happier for you. And then Michael came back and now this." She gently patted Sarah's hand in sympathy.

Sarah swallowed hard. "I'm sorry. I thought I was. I was so sure that he wouldn't come back. I was so ready to move on, and then, when he came back"—she threw up her hands—"we hung out and spent so much time together that by the time he'd left, I was hopelessly in love with him again. Right back where I started." The words were like a door slamming shut on her destiny. She would love Michael for the rest of her life, and there was nothing she could do about it. She could find a nice man, get married, and possibly fall in love with him. But it would never have the same depth as what she felt for Michael.

"I'm doomed," she whispered.

To her surprise, Juliet giggled. "Sarah, I love you, but you don't need to be so melodramatic. There are other fish in the sea. In fact, some are looking right at us."

Sarah lifted her head and glanced behind her. Two men waved from another table. Sarah grabbed Juliet's hand to stop her from waving back and marched her over to the heap of ski equipment they'd dropped before sitting down. "Oh no, you don't. Not this time. Fine, I'll go skiing."

"I always knew you could be reasonable," Juliet said. Sarah pulled a face at her friend; and Juliet laughed so hard, she had to plant her ski poles to keep her from keeling over. "Oh, Sarah."

Together, they climbed onto a ski lift that quickly took them to the top of the run. A blue one this time. It seemed that Juliet had not forgotten Sarah's promise to herself as much as Sarah would have wished she could.

"You ready for this?"

"Absolutely." Change was inevitable. Sarah just had to embrace it.

A day of skiing was everything Sarah needed. The wide-open spaces and the clear, blue sky and white snow moved things into perspective for her troubled heart. During the green run and taking her first try on the blue run, Sarah decided. Michael was gone again, and this time, she doubted he would be coming back to Snowy Springs. The constant throb of memories that ran into her every time she walked out her door made the decision all the easier. There was nothing that said it was too late to chase her dreams again.

If someone had told Michael when he returned stateside that the way to patch up the rip in his soul was mind-bending hard work, he'd have thought they were joking. And yet, with the combination of the restorations on the old church Levi pastored and the nightly talks with him, Michael could feel the fissure healing. He could feel sanity returning to his mind. It wasn't perfect, but it was a start.

Nights were still tricky, but after a serious discussion with the base psychiatrist and his family's intervention, he slept through the night more often than not. The bone weariness he'd carried since Kandahar was slowly melting off his shoulders. There was still a long path ahead, but he was taking it one step at a time. Michael stretched to work out the kinks from the previous day's labor. He grabbed his Bible and went to sit in the sunroom in Levi's house. It was his favorite spot, and dawn was his favorite time of day. In the past, he'd watched the dawn with world-weary eyes, now he saw it as a new opportunity to be someone he'd always wanted to be.

The paper flipped effortlessly under his fingers as he paged to the words of a verse known intimately to his heart. *"I took you from the ends of the earth, from its farthest corners I called you. I said, 'You are my servant'; I have chosen you and have not rejected you. So do not fear, for I am with you; do not be dismayed, for I am your God. I will strengthen you and help you; I will uphold you with my righteous right hand" (Isa. 41:9).*

Since he'd been back home, Michael had felt far off, like he'd been abandoned by God. Banished to the place of his imprisonment. Previously elusive answers suddenly sprang up before him like fountains bursting into a parched land. In the last few weeks, he'd done some serious soul searching, and it had all begun the night God had retaken a hold of him.

"How was your meeting at the base?" Levi asked.

"Same old, same old. Breathe, pray, wait, eat well, sleep—yada, yada, yada."

"Give it time, Michael. God is still working on you."

"Really, I don't feel anything at all—nothing except fear and pain. I don't want to do this anymore, Levi. I can't. I'm not strong enough."

Levi sighed. "You can do it. I have faith in you."

"I wish I did." Michael rolled over the bed and ignored the click of the door closing at his brother leaving. He wasn't going to get better. He would forever be lost in his memories.

He glanced up at his Bible in its prominent position beside him. Trembling, he sat up and cradled the book between his rough hands. God, help me.

And then, the impossible happened. A drop fell on the cover, then another until a trickle washed down the black leather. The storm raging inside him speared him like a man thrust into a rampant ocean, desperate to swim away from the rocks. The torrent pushed him, pounding him again and again until there was nothing left to do but let it break. Let the waves crash over him and drag him under. And then, there was silence; and a still, small Voice said, "My son, I love you."

God had him. He hadn't left. Michael curled into a ball, threw the covers over his head, and prayed for all he was worth.

The water washed away his old, dead life and brought a new, fresh one in its place. Instead of fighting the anxiety and fear that lingered with soldiers in his condition on his own, he now fought with the whole host of Heaven behind him. And they were winning.

Smiling to himself, he picked up the letter Levi had sent him on his return to Snowy Springs. He kept it as a reminder of where he'd come from and the progress he'd made. Levi had been right. God hadn't left Michael's side in those years in captivity. He'd been there for each drop of blood and lament in the night. The truth had broken him, but it had also set him free. Free from the bonds and lies of the one who planned for his eternal destruction.

"You're up early," Levi said and handed him a cup of coffee.

Michael took a sip and shrugged. "Dawn is the best time of the day. Reminds me to be grateful I'm alive." He saluted Levi with his mug, and Levi smiled.

"As are we. Have you made a decision?"

He and Levi had talked extensively about his next steps, what Michael wanted out of life. There was only one thing. His heart wished harder and harder for her each day. Sarah. His unresolved feelings for his best friend's sister plagued him with uncertainty until he'd finally admitted the truth that had been staring him in the face for months now. He was still in love with Sarah. It was his turn to put his pride in his pocket and beg her forgiveness. That was if she hadn't married Lucas already. Something told him she hadn't, that she'd been as cut up as he over his leaving. Then again, it could be his imagination or a bad case of wishful thinking.

"I think I'm going back." The decision sparked something inside him that swirled and moved until every cell and limb was warm.

Levi laughed. "Well, praise the Lord. He's finally seen the light." Once he'd gotten himself under control, Levi took the seat beside him. "Michael, I have a secret I've been meaning to tell you."

"Oh?"

"You're in love with Sarah Bakker."

"Yeah, I know."

"And I think you won't ever forgive yourself if you don't go and see what might come of that."

Michael nodded. "Funny, that's exactly what I was thinking."

They laughed. Michael marveled again at the sheer joy of laughing with lightness inside him.

"How soon?"

"In the next few days. I don't think Mom is going to let me go without a huge fuss. I might just take it slow to give her time to adjust to the idea."

Levi nodded. Michael came back a shadow of himself. In the time since, he'd become a new person—not the same one who'd left but one who'd grown and lived to tell the tale. One who, with the help of God, was slowly putting the pieces of his life back together. And hopefully, with Sarah by his side.

Chapter Twenty-Four

A wry smile lifted his cheek as he turned down the familiar street. In the time he'd been away, not much had changed in Snowy Springs, but the time had irrevocably changed him. Michael slowed and came to a stop outside the hardware store. Aaron talked animatedly to someone inside. Man, he owed him an apology or something. He'd really left him in the lurch. It couldn't have been helped, but it stunk anyway.

He sighed. Leave the past and embrace the present. Michael climbed out of the truck, careful to close the door behind him, and walked into the store. Aaron stopped midsentence and glanced at him. "Michael?"

Was he that unrecognizable? No, he doubted it. "Yep."

"Man, I don't know whether to be glad to see you or to punch you in the nose."

"I'll take either one." He deserved either one. The way he'd left things, anyone would be mad. His thoughts turned to Sarah—especially Sarah. She had more reason than the others.

Aaron studied him for a moment and heaved one big shoulder. "Nah, I figure you did that job pretty well yourself. It's good to see you, but what are you doing here?" He extended his hand out to Michael to shake.

Relieved, Michael grasped it and shook it. "I'm sorry, man. There was just so much—"

Aaron held up his hand and cut Michael off. "No explanations necessary."

Michael slid his hands into his pockets and studied something on the floor. "I came back." Mentally repeating what Levi had told him in the past weeks, Michael lifted his head and looked straight at his friend. "Everything isn't perfect, but it's better. Levi says time will heal all wounds. Well"—he chuckled—"at least make sure I can live with the memories."

Aaron nodded. "So, you're back for good then?"

"Yes, there is a lot of fixing up I have to do in Snowy Springs."

Aaron nodded, understanding who Michael meant. "She's not with Lucas anymore, if it makes any difference."

Surprise drew him up. "She's not?"

"Michael, I think me and you need to have a discussion that perhaps should have happened a long time ago." Aaron gestured to the apartment behind him. "I didn't do anything with the sofas, so . . ." He turned and walked toward the back of the store.

Michael took a deep inhale through his nose and braced himself. This could go two ways—either Aaron would give his blessing for Michael to pursue Sarah, or Aaron would politely tell Michael to stay away. Maybe it wouldn't be that polite if Michael resisted. Because he would, with everything he had. He had time and patience, but he would not walk away from Sarah again.

Michael climbed the dark stairs. Memories lingered in the empty recesses of the apartment. The laughter he'd shared with Sarah the day they'd gone skiing. A small smile lifted his cheek. He ached to see her. Closing his eyes, he sought peace and counted backward from ten. *Lord, please help him to understand.*

Aaron sat on one of the sofas and waited for him to sit down. The seat creaked quietly under his weight as he settled in. The air smelled dusty and empty, like no one had been in the apartment since he'd left. He wondered why that was.

"Listen, Michael, you're one of my oldest friends. But when it comes to Sarah . . . " He swallowed. "Did you know she's been in love with you since she was fifteen? She cried for months after you disappeared; and when I thought she could finally see the end of the tunnel, you came back."

Aaron stood and began to pace around the room. "I need to know that if you are back that you will leave her alone. Let her heart heal and find someone who can make her happy."

Guilt wove in his stomach, warring against his love for Sarah. He scrubbed his hair back. It was longer now than it had been for years. An overwhelming wave of sweet emotion crashed into his heart. She'd loved him for years. He'd thought he'd seen it a time a two when they were in high school but not once since, not until the night he'd given her the necklace. When he'd returned home after his captivity, things were different between them, and Lucas had been in the picture.

Michael frowned. He should've seen it. Sarah had shown it each and every time he'd seen her—how much she cared for him—and it wasn't just about the kisses they'd shared.

"Michael, did I lose you? Will you promise?" Aaron sank down into the sofa with a pained expression.

It was time to take another chance. "I can't make you that promise, Aaron. I love her." Truth and certainty circled his heart. Peace lingered there, too—ease at the end of a long, challenging journey and the assurance of finally coming home.

Aaron's eyes grew wide, and his mouth fell open. "You love her?"

Michael nodded. "Yes. I came to Snowy Springs to tell her, and now that she isn't with Lucas . . ."

Aaron's stiff shoulders visibly relaxed as a broad smile appeared on his face. "You're sure?"

Michael smiled. "Really? I tell you I love your sister, and you ask me if I'm serious? Tell me this: have I ever told you about a woman I loved?"

Aaron grinned. "There was that one girl in high school. What was her name . . . Bethany?"

He groaned. "Come on, man, you're killing me. Bethany had nothing on Sarah."

A loud laugh bellowed from the other side of the room. "That is possibly the best news I have heard today." Aaron glanced down at his phone. "I think I might be able to help you out with that. Sarah needs help at the church with the decorations. You in?"

Happiness filled his chest. "Are you kidding? Of course."

"Great, we have less than five minutes to get there."

The two men raced to the door laughing like schoolboys on the night of prom. Michael couldn't believe what had just happened. Things between him and Aaron were good, and now he was on his way to see Sarah. What could possibly go wrong?

The church building buzzed with activity. Everywhere, people busily moved around. Some packed boxes; others laughed as they gave directions; and some stood around talking. The familiar din made

Michael smile. This time being back in Snowy Springs felt different. It wasn't the people around him who were different. *He* was different.

He followed Aaron, who immediately sought out Lana. Aaron said something to her in a low murmur, and then a warm smile flashed in Michael's direction. Okay, maybe this forgiveness thing wouldn't be too bad. Lana wiped her hands on a dust cloth and walked over to him, enfolding him in a tight hug. "It's good to see you again, Michael. She's in the storeroom; you'd better hurry."

Stunned for a moment, Michael was speechless. Lana nodded again. "The storeroom, boy," she said in the way she used to when they were kids. "Be careful with my girl."

"I'll keep watch," Aaron said in a conspiratorial whisper.

"Yes, ma'am," he said.

He hurried to the storeroom. He took a moment to compose himself and then walked toward the door. There in the dim storeroom stood Sarah, a vast array of stuff around her feet. At first, she didn't see him, her focus on the clipboard in her hand. Michael leaned against the doorframe and just looked at her. He loved the way her brown hair swung a little bit below her shoulders and the cute way she frowned when she was concentrating. She quickly licked her lips, and Michael felt a flush rush up his skin. Oh, he loved those lips, too. Hopefully, he'd get a chance to kiss them again soon.

With a loud clearing of his throat, Michael walked deeper into the room and closed the door behind him. Lana had said there was an issue with the lock a few months ago, and Michael sincerely hoped they hadn't fixed it yet. Sarah started at the sound, like a rabbit caught in the headlights. She stared at him, and the clipboard clattered to the floor beside her. Waiting, caught in his trap. Time seemed endless as step by step, he closed the distance between them until the warmth of her body reached his.

"What are you doing here?" she demanded.

"I need to talk to you," he replied and stepped as close to her as he dared.

"Michael." Her hand cupped the necklace around her neck. Hope caught wing in his heart; if she still wore that necklace, maybe there was a chance.

"It reminds me of you," she said.

Michael swallowed. "I'd hoped it would," he said thickly.

The necklace twirled between her fingers. "But you said . . . " It was too much. He tentatively touched her hand with his and stilled its anxious movement. "I know what I said, Sarah. I lied."

Thinking quickly, he stepped back. "Is it true, Sarah?"

"Is what true?" she asked.

"What Aaron told me—is it true?"

Before she could utter any words, color rushed into her cheeks. "Would it make a difference if I said no?" she whispered.

He stalled. "Probably not."

Sarah swallowed hard, and Michael's pulse picked up. "Then why does it matter?"

That was the ultimate question, wasn't it, and it was now his turn to be honest. "It matters to me. Have you loved me for all those years?"

Sarah's gaze dropped to their entangled hands. She wrapped her right arm around her middle, but the other she left in his. "Yes."

The agony in her words ripped a hole in his heart. Joy so pure sailed through him. He hoped he'd get the chance to make things right with her. His heart couldn't stand her pain.

"Sarah." Her name slipped off his tongue like sweet incense as he closed the distance he'd created between them. Sarah stiffened. Michael hesitated and rested his hands on her hips. He wanted to crush her to him, hold her tightly forever, but he needed to be cautious. With painstaking slowness, he drew her stiff form closer. He sighed as she seemed to melt into him.

"Sarah, are you in here . . . " a voice said. The door slammed open and filled the room with a bright light. Aaron, Lana, and Juliet stood at the door; each wore varying expressions. Aaron and Lana were embarrassed, and Juliet, well, just looked ticked.

Sarah stepped away from him. "If you'll excuse me . . . " She practically ran to Juliet, and the two disappeared around the corner, whispering furiously.

"Sorry, I tried to stop her," Aaron said.

Michael rubbed the back of his neck. "It's okay, I have all the time in the world for Sarah. I'll just have to try again." No matter how long or how much it took, he would win Sarah back.

Chapter Twenty-Five

"Was that who I think it was?" Juliet asked.

Sarah gripped her hands together to keep them from shaking and nodded. "Yeah, it's Michael."

"That man has a lot of nerve coming back here after the way he hurt you." Juliet was in full protective mode. Sarah loved her for it. Although she didn't feel the same indignation Juliet was displaying on her behalf, oddly, she was relieved.

When Michael's gaze had met hers, those blue eyes she loved were clear. The pain and desperation she'd seen the night before he'd left were absent, replaced by something that looked like peace. Her heart ached for him, but she couldn't trust any emotion she experienced when it came to Michael. He'd hurt her, and she was not about to let herself in for round two.

They hurried to the car and drove off to the community center. The Christmas pageant would take place the next night. Yesterday, Aaron and his crew had finally managed to complete the roof. The ground crew had replaced the ceilings in the other rooms, and despite the lateness, the community center was ready to be decorated. Being the small community it was, the entire Snowy Springs community had come to lend a hand in decorating and setting up.

Sarah balanced a box on her hip and lugged it to the stage that headed the long room. It smelled like fresh paint with a hint of wood, and she admired Aaron's work for a moment. She was truly blessed to have her family. She'd be lost without them.

"Can I help you with that?" Michael asked and reached to take the box from her.

"No, I got it, thanks."

His shoulders drooped. "I guess I deserved that."

"What are you talking about?" she asked. The box on her hip began to slip, and she shifted to hold it better.

Michael came into her personal space. "Just give me the box, Sarah."

She handed it over, and they walked to the stage, where Michael set it down.

"Can we talk?" he asked.

"Michael, I . . . I can't do this right now."

Michael sighed. "Sarah, please . . . I wasn't myself. There was so much going on. But that's . . . well, not in the past but better."

Sarah turned to him. "Michael, you seem better, and I'm really happy for you. I will always value your friendship." The half-truths spilled out of her like water, her heart protesting each and every one.

Michael's smile turned tender. "You're going to make me work for it, aren't you?"

"Work for what?" Sarah asked.

A mysterious light entered his eyes. "I've got nothing but time."

Had he always spoken in riddles? Sarah shook her head as she watched Michael walk away. He whistled softly, and if she didn't know any better, there was a little spring in his step—intolerable man.

Marveling at the confusion Michael still managed to make her feel, Sarah unpacked the decorations and began placing them around the stage. The tree seemed to be as stubborn as she was tonight and took a few good yanks before eventually breaking free of the netting. It wobbled precariously, and then with a loud thump, it stilled inside the pot. Sarah rubbed her hands together and began to wrestle a long string of white lights. Who knew tree decorating could be this perilous?

A few moments later, Michael appeared with another box. He placed it beside the others and then began to help her decorate the large tree.

"Your mother invited me to the family Christmas Eve party," he said nonchalantly.

"Oh, how nice of her. I'm sure you'll enjoy an old-fashioned Snowy Springs Christmas."

Michael chuckled at her snippy tone. Honestly, the man was making her head spin. What did he want with her, and why was he so persistent about it? She would've hoped he'd gotten the message when she'd unceremoniously brushed him off. But there were two things she'd always known about Michael: he was as stubborn as a donkey and as persistent as a bulldog. And now, for some reason she couldn't fathom, he had focused those qualities on her.

Michael arranged another string of tinsel. Sarah rolled her eyes and quietly stepped behind and rearranged it. He hung a few more ornaments; again, Sarah repositioned them. Then she heard a slight snicker, and she turned to face him. Michael smiled broadly. His shoulders shook with amusement.

"You're doing that on purpose, aren't you?" she asked wryly as she crossed her arms over her chest.

"Maybe." He slid his hands into his pockets, at ease. His blues danced, and he smiled with such satisfaction that she wanted to smack him. Something tickled her memory. It grew and grew until it swept over her. The Michael she'd known her whole life stood before her. The same boyish mannerism, the same teasing spirit. And she still couldn't have him.

Accepting the inevitable, she continued to decorate side by side with Michael. No matter what he had done to her or said to her, her love for him was sealed. The thought brought a tremor to her lips, and she swallowed back the wave of emotion that threatened to engulf her.

At that moment, Michael glanced over at her. The tenderness she saw there made her heart stutter and stall. "I think I need to help Juliet with the boxes," she said at last.

Michael nodded and continued to decorate the tree. Sarah glanced over her shoulder as she walked back to the car. Michael was watching her, his hand poised above a box. As if feeling her gaze, he winked and dug into the container for another decoration. Heart racing, Sarah came to a stop outside the community center. She leaned against the truck and allowed the frigid air to clear her scrambled thoughts. Michael had, once again, without any apparent effort, thrown her life into turmoil. And she wasn't quite sure how she felt about it.

The Christmas Eve pageant had finally arrived. The last set of ballet dancers pirouetted around the community center stage. Soft strains of *The Nutcracker* filled the room in a crescendo of leaps and twirls. It always amazed Sarah the grace with which ballet dancers seemed to move. Their delicate tutus and white and black gauzy costumes moving elegantly with each step.

Her heart was full. The Christmas pageant had been an enormous success. Everything had come together with such remarkable fluidity that sometimes she didn't understand how it had all happened. She glanced over to the seated crowd, her eyes involuntarily searching for him like they always did. *You're a hopeless case, girl.* And she always would be when it came to him.

With a flash of multicolored lights and a rising chorus, the dance came to an end. Applause arose from the audience in a wave of sound. Juliet squeezed her shoulder.

"You did it," she said.

"We did it."

"Yeah, but you did most of it. Come on, Sarah, give credit where credit is due."

"Okay, yes." She squealed. "We did it."

Juliet laughed and hugged her as they danced in a small circle in the wings of the stage. Jerry Finn, one of the dancers, came up to her and handed her a long-stemmed red rose. Sarah took it and inhaled its glorious scent.

"Thank you. Is this from you?"

Jerry shook his head and silently walked away.

Juliet studied the rose. "Who do you think that's from?"

"Probably Aaron. He likes to remind me to celebrate small wins. Like tonight."

"That's sweet," Juliet said. "Anyway, hun, I have to get going. Callen is down with a cold, and, well, tomorrow is Christmas. I don't know how I'm going to manage with all the family and him out of commission."

Sarah hugged her friend again. "Thank you for everything, Juliet."

With a soft "you're welcome," Juliet said goodnight.

It had been a beautiful afternoon, and now she needed to hurry over to her mother's house. Leaving the cleaning and closing to the rest of the committee, Sarah quickly grabbed her coat and rushed to her car.

The drive to Lana's house was ten minutes from the community center. Sarah chewed her bottom lip. Would Michael come? How did she feel if he did? She should've told Aaron she couldn't come, made up some excuse. He would know she was lying and would ask, and then she'd have to say to him that of course she was still in love with Michael. And that would lead to its own set of problems.

Groaning, Sarah flexed her hands against her steering wheel. Michael and his gorgeous eyes and smile. The house came into view, and Sarah pulled to a stop behind her mom's SUV. Cheery Christmas lyrics sang from the place. Okay, it was now or never.

Help me out here, please, Lord.

Sarah climbed out of the car and entered the battle.

"Glad you could make it," her mother said and closed the door behind her.

"Me, too. The weather is crazy out there. Did the weather channel predict the snow tonight?" Sarah took off her coat and hung it up, fluffed her hair, and sank her cold feet into warm bunny slippers waiting for her at the door. The smell of apple pie and roasting turkey swirled around her.

"No, the snow was supposed to come tomorrow."

"As unpredictable as always." Sarah laughed, glad to be safe and dry in her mother's house. Her relief was short-lived as Michael came into the room.

"Hey, Sarah," he said.

Her heart stuttered in her chest. The battle was already lost. Could she hold on?

"Uh, hi. Mom, if you don't mind, I'll go see if Aaron needs any help with the fire." Sarah laid her gloves beside her purse and darted to the living room. As she brushed past him, she could have sworn that Michael sighed. Oh, well.

Aaron stood beside the fire, Dakota at his shoulder. He directed her on ways to place the firewood; both of them laughed. Sarah leaned against the door frame. Her brother was in love. It was evident in the way his head inclined toward her, the gentle smile that teased his lips, and his total entrancement with Dakota.

"Hey, sis, how's it going?"

"Hi, Sarah. Are you okay?" Dakota hugged her quickly, her brow creased in concern.

"Aaron's been telling stories again, has he?"

A warm presence came to stand close beside her, his shoulder brushing her. Aaron glanced beside her, his eyebrow raised. Michael muttered something.

"Fine," she squeaked. Her brain had taken a vacation.

Dakota smiled as Aaron wrapped his arm around her waist and tugged her into his side, kissing Dakota loudly on the cheek. Sarah glanced at Michael. He glanced back. They shared a silent moment much like they had growing up when Aaron was acting strange. The amusement in his eyes slowly faded into something else, and Sarah's stomach filled with butterflies.

"Sarah, can we talk? I just need a minute," Michael said softly.

"Listen to him, Squirt," Aaron joined in.

Hurt stiffened her spine. "Just leave me alone, both of you."

Again, she found herself dashing away. Maybe she should find somewhere to hide. Her heart couldn't take any more of this.

Chapter Twenty-Six

It was quiet out here. The falling snow blocked out the happy sounds that came from the house behind her. Sarah hunched her shoulders against the cold. Why she'd thought it was a good idea to go outside without her coat was beyond her, but she'd needed to leave. To get away from his presence. The pain was too much, and she could feel herself bleeding each time their eyes met across the room.

With a trembling hand, she wiped a tear that slid down her cheek. It was no use. Love was meant to be something happy and exciting, not painful and sad. The sound of laughter flooded the darkness as the screen door swished open and closed. Probably her mother coming to check on her again. Mama knew. She always had.

Sarah wrapped her arms tighter around her middle and wished she'd remembered her coat. The warm wool wouldn't heat the hole inside of her, the place where, from the time she was fifteen years old, Michael had wormed into it and made a place there. Her tears continued to fall, and she swallowed hard against the sobs that threatened to break the stillness of the night.

Lord, is this all there is for me? To love a man who played with her heart? She'd been so sure she was over him. From the moment she'd laid eyes on Michael in the restaurant, something dormant in her had come alive. She'd fought tooth and nail to get him out, but it hadn't helped because when she'd given her heart to Michael, even though he'd never known, it had been forever.

"Sarah?" Warm hands wrapped her coat over her cold shoulders, encouraged her stiff arms into the sleeves, and wrapped the folds around her body. She immediately sank into the warm depths of down surrounding her. "What are you doing out here? You'll catch your death."

Michael. Couldn't he just leave her alone? Didn't he know how hard this was for her?

"Sarah." This time, his voice was closer. Shaking hands held onto her hips and turned her around to face him. He dropped them just as quickly.

Sarah kept her head down, wiping at the remaining tears running down her cheeks. He wouldn't see her cry, never again. A white tissue appeared before her. She took it and cleaned her face. "Thanks," she whispered.

Michael sighed loudly. "Sarah, would you please look at me?"

She shook her head; it was too painful. "Go back inside, Michael. Enjoy the party. I'll be fine."

Sarah turned and walked deeper into the forested area behind her mother's house. Why wouldn't he just leave her alone?

"Sarah." A firm hand grasped her elbow and spun her around. Her hands landed on his solid chest. Frustration sparked in his ocean-deep gaze.

"What do you want, Michael?" she said at last. If he was going to break her heart again, he might as well get it done so that he could leave and she could once again mourn in private.

"You." Without eloquence, the word was said with such honesty that it stunned Sarah into silence.

Michael chuckled. She didn't see anything funny. As if directed by some soft symphony, Michael lifted his hand to her cheek and settled the other on her waist. He pulled her to him again. His thumb slowly traced the top of her cheek before it lightly touched her lips. He smiled as he slid a strand of hair behind her ear, leaving a warm trail along her skin. Her eyes threatened to flutter closed against the touch. His blue eyes softened; his mouth still held a whisper of a smile.

"Sarah, my sweet Sarah, how could I have ever hurt you?" His words whispered against the skin of her cheek, his facial hair brushing it with each word. Her knees turned to liquid, and she braced her hand against his forearms.

"Michael, what—"

"Sarah." He paused and took a deep breath, watching her intently as if searching for something. "I love you, Sarah."

"Michael, please don't mess with me." She sighed. "I can't take anymore." How could it be? He'd told her he wasn't capable of love with anyone anymore. He muttered something under his breath.

"What did you say?" she asked.

"I said, then I guess I'll just have to prove it to you."

"Wha—" His mouth silenced hers. The kiss was one like she'd never experienced. Soft lips moved against hers, tender, loving. Each brush of his mouth silently confirming, again and again, his love for her. Love streamed over her heart as, kiss by kiss, Michael healed all he'd destroyed in the past weeks.

"I'm sorry, Sarah," he said, finally releasing her from their intense embrace.

Her body shook with blissful emotion. He loved her. Did she love him enough to accept his love? To chance her heart again?

Michael smiled, a slight frown bending his brow. "I think we need to talk honestly for once."

The swing at the end of the garden creaked as they settled into its soft seat. Michael reached for the blanket on the seat and laid it over them. He curled his arm around her shoulders and took her other hand in his. He tenderly ran his fingers over hers. Was that contentment she saw? Perhaps mingled in with happiness? Whatever it was, Michael wore the expression well, and it softened the harsh planes of his face. A tremble passed through his solid frame. Sarah wanted to hold him close, make the pain go away, but she waited. She'd laid all she had on the line before, and Michael had rejected her.

Michael looked up from their hands, his expression troubled, a faraway look in his eyes. "Before I left for that deployment, I knew I was in love with you. But I was afraid. I was leaving, and I had no idea if I would be back. When my squad was captured by those insurgents, I made myself hard. I had to. I had to convince myself not to feel anything because if I did for one moment, they would break me." His fingers convulsed unwillingly around hers. He swallowed harshly.

"When I came back stateside, I had no idea what to expect. I'd been away for so long, everything had changed. And I convinced myself that I was incapable of feeling any kind of soft emotion. The nightmares constantly reminded me of why I was like that. I wasn't at peace, but I accepted that it was the way things would be. The way they had to be. And then I saw you at that restaurant, and all those well-determined rules I'd made for myself suddenly seemed wrong. You were like a meteor that came crashing into the darkness, forcing the walls to burst open."

He smiled self-consciously, his pain and confusion plain in his vulnerable eyes. Sarah leaned forward and placed her lips on his. It was reassurance, and it was love.

"I love you," she whispered.

"And I love you," he said, enfolding her in his arms.

Sarah settled her head against Michael's shoulder, content to let her love rest with him. His head rested on top of hers. He rocked the swing forward and back with his legs.

"That night at the rodeo scared the life out of me. I could see Aaron trying to help, but I couldn't stop it. I wasn't in control. I was trapped in a nightmare. And your voice was the only sound that reached me in the chaos. It called to me. I focused on your voice with all I had left, and at last, the nightmare retreated. I'm sorry, Sarah. I didn't want to hurt you, but I knew the possibility of that happening again . . . " His voice trailed off as he fought for composure.

"It's okay. Now that I understand, it makes sense why you pushed me away." The swing shifted again as she pushed herself up to face him. Michael's head was bowed over their entwined hands, his jaw clenched.

"Michael," she said and lifted his face to meet hers. "You know I have loved you from an age where I barely knew what love was and every day after that." Michael's expression softened. "And I will continue to love you every day still. Let me fight this battle with you. Let me pray with you, rejoice with you, and stand by you when the darkness is overwhelming."

Arms seized her and pulled her closer as hungry lips met hers again. "Sarah, I love you. This might be a bit soon, but how long before you'd agree to marry me?"

"Today, if you asked."

A slow smile with a hint of mischief appeared. "I was hoping you would say that."

"Hoping?"

Smoothly, Michael switched their places, her on the swing, him on bended knee before her. He held out a small, black box in his trembling hand.

"Sarah Bakker, I love you, and from the first time I knew you were special to me as a bumbling soldier to the man kneeling before you now, I have wanted you to be in my life. I know you're the one for me. Your kindness, love, and generous heart have helped me begin healing that, Lord willing, will continue, and your smile brings light to my darkness. Will do me the honor of being my wife?"

Joy so intense and so sweet spread through Sarah. Michael loved her and wanted her for his wife. *Thank You, Lord.* "Yes, with my whole heart, yes."

Laughing, Michael pulled her up from the seat and sealed the promise in a passionate kiss. "Thank You, Lord," he whispered against her mouth and kissed her again.

"I assume she said yes?" Aaron stood in the doorway leading into the back of the house, his one arm around Dakota, the other held out to Michael.

"Yes, she did. Now, go back inside, so I can give her a ring."

"Did someone say *ring*?" Her mother hustled out of the house, her red apron gripped between her hands.

"Oh, Mama, I got a ring. He finally asked me to marry him."

"Took you long enough, my boy. I thought you were going to make our girl wait for eternity."

"No, ma'am, I may be slow, but I ain't stupid." Sarah raised an eyebrow. "Okay, most of the time."

"Can I see the ring?" her mother asked, grabbing her hand.

"If you would quit distracting me, I'd like to get it on her hand before she changes her mind."

"Unlikely." And Sarah had to agree.

Michael took her hand in his and slid the beautiful diamond ring onto her finger. "Forever," he whispered and kissed her.

"That's all I'm asking for."

The End

Coming Next From Michelle Dykman

The Deal with Dakota

Could his deal be the one to make her stay?

Dakota Manning is on the run after years of abuse at the hands of her boyfriend, Bobby. Her desperate flight comes to an abrupt end outside the small town of Snowy Springs. With her car broken and with nowhere to go, Dakota suddenly finds herself in need of employment and a place to stay. Aaron Bakker, the town's hardware store owner, offers her a deal—a place to stay and a way to pay for the repairs to her car in exchange for helping him out at his store.

The Deal with Dakota is a story of hope, reconciliation, and leaving the past behind, and is a sweet reminder that even the biggest mistakes can be forgiven.

For more information about
Michelle Dykman
&
If Only In My Dreams
please visit:

www.michelledykman.com

Ambassador International's mission is to magnify the Lord Jesus Christ and promote His Gospel through the written word.

We believe through the publication of Christian literature, Jesus Christ and His Word will be exalted, believers will be strengthened in their walk with Him, and the lost will be directed to Jesus Christ as the only way of salvation.

For more information about
AMBASSADOR INTERNATIONAL
please visit:

www.ambassador-international.com

Thank you for reading this book. Please consider leaving us a review on your favorite retailer's website, Goodreads or Bookbub, or our website.

Elaine Smith is content with her life as a widow in the small, coastal town of Sabal Palms. She enjoys her time with friends, and she enjoys writing stories and devotionals, despite the advice of her friends. When a southern squall hits the coast, Elaine's abandoned writings start showing up in the most mysterious places. Can God actually use Elaine's trash to become someone else's treasure? Is there more to her writings than she even realizes?

When Dr. Sam Gray is sent to Africa as a volunteer physician, he is counting down the days until he can go home again. During a trip to the local school, he runs into the Cloverdales, a missionary family determined to win every soul to Christ. Try as he might, Dr. Sam can't seem to resist the family and finds himself being pulled into their midst again and again. As he battles his own beliefs, Dr. Sam begins to find that maybe he's in need of a Physician as well. Can anyone heal his hardened heart?

Sam Anthem has always been a team player, leading his Home Team on secret missions around the world. When he is forced on a vacation, he is introduced to a former covert ops soldier-turned pastor. But the vacation takes a turn when the Home Team comes under attack. As the team fights to stay alive against an unknown adversary, Sam begins to wonder if there is more to life than just the job. With his life on the line, Sam must decide between the job or his newfound faith and possible love.